The Rancher's Unwelcome Christmas Bride

Cheryl Wright

Copyright

THE RANCHER'S UNWELCOME CHRISTMAS BRIDE
(Unwelcome Brides Series)

Copyright ©2024 by Cheryl Wright

Dedication

To Margaret Tanner, my very dear friend and fellow author, for her enduring encouragement and friendship.

To Alan, my husband of almost fifty years, who has been a relentless supporter of my writing and dreams for many years.

To You, my wonderful readers, who encourage me to continue writing these stories. It is such a joy knowing so many of you enjoy reading my stories as much as I love writing them for you.

Table of Contents

Chapter One 5

Chapter Two 10

Chapter Three 17

Chapter Four 29

Chapter Five 34

Chapter Six 42

Chapter Seven 49

Chapter Eight 56

Chapter Nine 62

Chapter Ten 68

Chapter Eleven 76

Chapter Twelve 83

Chapter Thirteen 91

Chapter Fourteen 97

Chapter Fifteen 103

Chapter Sixteen 108

Chapter Seventeen 113

Epilogue 117

From the Author 123

About the Author 124

Links 125

Chapter One

Mountain View, Montana – 1880s

The sudden jerking of the wagon woke Emma Seymour from a deep sleep.

"Whoa!" The unfamiliar masculine voice startled her. She glanced about, but it was too dark – she couldn't fathom where she was. "Blasted snow," the same voice said, this time sounding irritated.

Emma stiffened as she remembered where she was and the circumstances that led her there. She closed her eyes, but it didn't erase the memory of that awful day. Now her entire body shook. And it wasn't because of the cold.

Without warning, it all came flooding back. If she were honest, Emma would prefer she forgot. Having the entire situation wiped from her memory would be a godsend, but she knew it would never happen. Instead, she needed to face the truth. The memory of what she had witnessed would always remain embedded in her mind.

She took a fortifying breath as the wagon moved again.

Emma did not know who the wagon belonged to – she only knew it was in the right place at the right time to ensure her escape.

Where she would end up was anyone's guess. Emma silently prayed she would be safer wherever it was. Her life was in imminent danger, and she knew full well if she'd stayed back in Blacktown, she would be dead by now.

"Gid-yup!" The male voice came through loud and clear, and Emma pondered poking her head outside the canvas. Then she talked herself out of it. What if someone caught sight of her and recognized her?

Except that was nonsense. If the driver had to stop to clear snow, which she assumed, it meant they were on an isolated road. She only hoped he lived somewhere isolated. Somewhere where no one could find her. A place to hide away until it was safe to show her face again.

The road was far more bumpy than she'd expected, and Emma was suddenly flung upwards until she hit the top of the canvas. "Ow!" she said, then slapped a hand to her mouth. She prayed the driver did not hear her. There was surely enough noise from the horses and the road to cover her words?

They continued on their journey, and her pounding heart slowed. Emma had no idea where she was headed, but she believed it had to be safer than where she'd come from.

~*~

The constant movement of the wagon had lulled Emma into a deep sleep. She'd barely slept for days, always on alert, always ensuring she was safe. Now she opened her eyes, glancing about, but all she saw were boxes.

She ached all over. The floor of the wagon was most uncomfortable. Especially sleeping there. Emma had to stop herself from groaning. The last thing she wanted was to reveal herself.

At least she had slept a little. Those last few days on the stagecoach had been grueling. Trying to sleep upright was difficult. Being surrounded by strangers was even more so. Emma did not know who she could trust and who she couldn't. As much as she wanted to close her eyes and go to sleep, she'd forced herself to stay awake.

Changing routes every day was difficult, but she needed to cover her tracks. Emma's heart pounded again as the wagon came to a stop.

"I hope it was a pleasant trip, Boss," another unfamiliar voice said.

"It was uneventful, Gus, which is the best I can hope for." This was the same person who had driven the wagon, Emma was certain. He sounded kind. Why she thought that, Emma didn't know, but his voice had her drawn to him. "Coffee first," he said, then the two men's voices seemed to fade away.

Emma decided to stay put. At least for now. She had no intention of putting herself into further danger, although she may have done that by stowing away on the man's wagon. There was a time when she trusted people. After her recent experience, Emma no longer trusted anyone.

The voices faded into oblivion. Perhaps it was now safe to leave the wagon? Emma tentatively opened the canvas on the back of the wagon. Only a smidgeon, though – she wanted to ensure the coast was clear. She couldn't see anyone, but her plan to find a place to hide seemed to vanish. Without showing herself, all Emma could see was a large barn. Perhaps she should make her way there?

Without another thought, that's exactly what she did.

Her heart pounded as she carefully climbed out of the wagon. Lightheaded after having laid down for what seemed an eternity, Emma tread carefully as she struggled through the snow to the barn.

Once inside, she glanced around. It seemed there were plenty of places to hide, but the loft seemed the obvious choice, as she would be harder to spot. She carefully climbed the wooden ladder and only relaxed once she was out of sight. Her situation was still precarious – the loft held nothing but hay.

How she would survive, Emma didn't know. Having to leave her possessions behind was gut-wrenching, but there was no choice. Fleeing at a moment's notice meant she had to leave immediately.

She'd survived until now, but Emma wondered how much longer she had to live. She was not confident of her chances of survival.

Chapter Two

"Time to unpack the wagon, Gus," Marcus Tyler said. "If you can spare the time, that is."

Marcus usually went to town once a month for supplies. Today was no different. The wagon was full to the brim. There was little space left, and it would take some time for the two men to get everything out and pack it all away. That was the worst of his monthly trips.

Both men stepped out of the ranch house and began their descent down the few steps. "Boss, wait," Gus said, reaching for his gun. He didn't say another word, only pointed.

"Hmmm," Marcus said, not giving anything away. The footprints in the snow meant they might have a chance of finding whoever was wandering around his property without permission. "They're small," he whispered.

"Like a child?" Gus asked.

Marcus shook his head. "Maybe." The two men followed the trail, which led to the barn. The horses were not riled up, so whoever it was had left them alone.

Every step he took felt like lead to Marcus. The snow was not deep, only a thin layer. Still, it was enough for the two men to follow, and hopefully find the intruder. As they stepped into the barn, Marcus knew they were walking into the unknown.

The ranch had been his home for Marcus's entire life. In fact, he was born there. He couldn't recall another time there had been an intruder. It made his heart pound with anticipation, and he considered the outcome.

Gus had his gun at the ready, but Marcus decided they were dealing with a child who had wandered off the beaten path. His gun stayed holstered. At least for now.

He glanced about, but saw no sign of where their young intruder had gone beyond the confines of the large barn. The horses seemed a little restless, but it could be they wanted Marcus to visit with them. He ignored their pleas, for now at least.

Looking up at the loft, he signaled to Gus that's where he was going. Before he began the short climb, he ran his fingers along the rungs of the ladder. It wasn't blatantly obvious at a glance, but the moisture on the rungs told Marcus all he needed to know.

Whoever was on his property had climbed the ladder. He pointed upwards and began the slow climb. Slow because he was trying to be as quiet as he could. Marcus didn't want to alert the trespasser of their presence.

The essence of surprise was on his side, and he hoped it meant less of a fight. The last thing Marcus wanted was to startle a child. There had to be a reason he, or she, had sought refuge on his property.

Upon reaching the top rung, Marcus peeked over the top and stared. What he found there was far from what he expected.

"Miss. Miss," Marcus said, trying to wake the sleeping woman. She'd made a bed for herself in the hay. Sleeping that way was far from comfortable. "Wake up, Miss," he said. This time, he gently shook her shoulder.

Slowly, her eyes opened, and two big brown eyes stared at him. "Oh!" she said, as if she was surprised to have been discovered. Marcus couldn't help but smile. She was far from the small child he'd expected.

It was then it hit him – how did she get here? The footprints began at the wagon. Did that mean…? Marcus slapped himself mentally. He must have carried her in the back of the wagon without knowing. If he'd unpacked when they arrived home, he would have found her earlier. Instead, he indulged in a hot coffee.

It was done now, and nothing he could do to change the past. "What are you doing here?" he demanded, instantly regretting his tone when her eyes filled with tears.

Instead of pursuing the information he needed, Marcus pulled her into his arms and consoled the stranger before him. She didn't resist, but he knew he'd crossed a line. She rested her head on his chest, and her arms slid around his waist. Tears ran down her face.

Whatever drove her to hide in the cold, uncomfortable loft, he didn't know. What Marcus knew was this woman, whoever she may be, needed protection. Otherwise, she wouldn't have hidden in this way.

His heart hammered in his chest. Having a woman on the property was the last thing he wanted. It would be too distracting. Not only for him, but also for his men. "You can stay tonight, but then you must leave," he told her firmly, but this time with less volume.

She wiped away the tears and pulled out of his arms. "Thank you," she whispered.

Marcus stared at her, trying to assess her situation. "What is your name?" he asked gently. "I am Marcus Tyler. This is my ranch," he said.

"I…I'm E..Emma," she said, sounding unsure of herself.

Marcus wondered what she was hiding. She gave away so little, and from where he stood, it seemed Emma, if that was really her name, didn't want to disclose her true identity. It didn't get past him she'd not given Marcus her surname.

The woman definitely had something to hide. Should he make it his business to find out what it was before she left in the morning? Marcus thought not. He didn't invite her here, and he didn't want Emma here.

He was doing just fine without having a woman intrude on his peaceful life.

~*~

Miss Emma Seymour – she'd finally declared her surname – sat quietly in Marcus's sitting room, as close to the fire as she could get.

Marcus did not doubt she would be cold, and offered her a blanket to help her warm up more quickly. "Thank you," she whispered before he'd finished draping the thick woolen blanket over her.

She looked tired. Marcus felt for her. He really did. But why Emma Seymour believed it was fine for her to stow away in his wagon and hide in his barn loft, he did not know. He didn't need this sort of disruption. He really didn't.

He didn't want a woman on his property, either. Marcus closed his eyes as he took a long and fortifying breath. Her presence was not wanted. *She* was not wanted. What he was supposed to do with her, Marcus didn't know. It was clear she was in some sort of trouble, but what that was, he didn't know.

Nor did he want to know.

He watched her over the rim of his mug. She took dainty sips of tea between mouthfuls of store-bought cake. She was hungry, that much was clear. It made him wonder how long it had been between meals. "I apologize about the cake," he said, and genuinely meant it. "I bought it from the mercantile."

She glanced across the table at him. "Does your housekeeper not bake for you?" Without warning, Emma slapped her hands to her mouth. "I'm sorry. It's none of my business."

He watched as her cheeks turned a pretty pink. It made him smile. "I don't have a housekeeper," he said.

"You need one," Gus said firmly. He then turned to their unwanted guest. "I've been telling him so for as long as I can remember."

Marcus glared at his foreman. It might be the truth, but it didn't mean he should announce it to this stranger. She might be pretty, but she was an unknown element, and who knows what she would do?

Emma Seymour licked her lips, and Marcus's heart fluttered. If he did nothing else this week, he had to get this woman out of his home.

"Here's an idea," Gus said, his lips curled upwards. "Miss Seymour could take on your housekeeping duties." He raised his eyebrows in question.

If the suggestion had been made in private, with just the two men present, it wouldn't have been so bad. Except that's not what Gus did, and now Marcus felt obligated. How would he get out of this predicament? Marcus had no idea.

He shook his head slightly and Gus stared at him. Daring him to refuse. Emma stared at him in anticipation, which was clearly what Gus was hoping for. Not only had his foreman been pushing him toward getting a housekeeper, he'd also suggested Marcus need a bride. That would never happen. Marcus was happily single.

Life was far more simple that way.

Chapter Three

Emma stared across the table at the two men. The foreman, Gus, seemed to be joking, and Marcus Tyler didn't like it one bit. Did that mean he would turn her over to the sheriff? She hoped not. The sheriff would lock her up. No doubt on orders from Sheriff Tommy Yates back in Blacktown.

She was certain Tommy would be spreading lies about her already. He was the one who killed those people, not Emma, but as their sheriff, he was revered by the good citizens of Blacktown. That meant they would trust him more than her.

Only Emma knew him better than anyone. They'd grown up together. Emma always knew there was evil surrounding him, even when they were both children. But as an adult, that evil had truly surfaced. She'd made it a point to never find herself alone with Tommy, because who knew what would happen?

She had simply been in the wrong place at the wrong time. As she'd turned the corner, Emma had witnessed Tommy kill four men. They didn't stand a chance, since the so-called sheriff had shot each one in the back.

Why he'd done that, she had no idea. Nor did she wait around to find out. She'd run as fast as she could, and hightailed it out of there. As luck would have it, the stagecoach was about to leave town.

"Did you hear what I said, Emma?" Marcus's voice pulled her out of her thoughts.

Wiping errant tears from her eyes, she glanced up at him. "I…I didn't. I'm sorry."

He sighed and took a mouthful of his coffee. "I asked if you knew how to cook."

Emma's heartbeat increased. Did that mean he was letting her stay? At least for tonight? "I do," she answered, hoping it wasn't some cruel joke he was playing.

She swallowed down the last of her tea and proceeded to choke on it. The rancher stood and came around to pound her back. Finally, her dignity returned, and she also stood. Until now, she hadn't realized how tall he was.

"Follow me," Marcus said firmly, then took her through the spacious kitchen and into the pantry. "You should find everything you need in here. Our supplies have been replenished today." He stared down into her face, not taking his eyes off her. Emma now realized that's what he'd been doing in town when she climbed into his wagon. "The root cellar is down here," he said, then showed her the entrance. "You can find milk, cheese, butter, and meat there. Do you feel up to cooking tonight?" he asked as they returned to the kitchen.

Did she? Not really, but if that's what it took to secure her place in this household, then it's exactly what she would do. "How many am I cooking for?" she asked, her mind already trying to figure out what she would make, given the time of day already.

"Six, including yourself." Marcus guided her back into the kitchen and opened a few cupboards, pointing out where everything was kept. "Come with me, and I'll show you where you'll sleep," he said, slight irritation in his voice.

Emma understood he'd asked her under duress, but that wasn't her fault. He stood at the door to a smallish room and waved her inside. "Is your bag up in the loft?" he asked.

She shook her head. "I have nothing. I had to flee for my life," she said, then slapped her hands to her mouth.

He stared at her. Emma stared back. It was akin to a standoff, with both parties not wanting to be the first to give in.

"Right, Boss," Gus said. "The wagon is now empty, so I'm off. I still have some chores to do." He turned and walked away, and Emma wondered what would happen next.

~*~

She had only moments earlier finished setting the table when the men filed into the house. Each one removed their boots and hat and left them at the door. At least that meant she wouldn't be dealing with savages.

"Miss Seymour," Gus said with a nod to his head. "This is Buck, Jay, and Cody." He pointing to each one as he named them. "We're looking forward to your cooking."

Emma's heart pounded. As much as she could cook, good old-fashioned cooking was her style. It would keep their bellies full, but there would be no fancy meals.

"Nice to meet you all," she said, then turned back to the stove momentarily. When she turned around again, the men were all still standing. Surely they weren't waiting for her to sit down? "Please," she said firmly, "sit down. Supper will be ready shortly."

Emma realized she was nervous about cooking for these strangers. She did not know what their expectations were, but would failure result in her being banished?

Giving the fried potatoes and onions a last stir, she pulled the pancakes out of the oven. Emma divided the pancakes between the six of them, then did the same with the potatoes and onions. The aroma wafted through the kitchen, and she worried it wouldn't be substantial enough. Unfortunately, she had limited time as she had been assigned the task of making supper late in the day.

As she handed out the food, she noticed her boss, Marcus, was not seated at the table. It was then the door opened, then quickly slammed shut. "Sorry I'm late," he said, kicking off his boots and leaving his hat at the door. He went straight to the counter and offered to help deliver the meals.

"I can do that," Emma whispered.

Marcus stared down at her. "So can I," he whispered back, then grabbed the last two plates waiting to be served.

As she sat down, Emma noticed all five men lean forward and take in the aroma. She glanced around the table. Each one looked as though they'd not eaten pancakes before.

"It smells delicious, Miss Seymour," Gus told her.

Emma's biggest wish was it tasted as good as it smelled. It had been a long time since she'd made pancakes. If they were at least passable, she would be happy. "Thank you, Gus," she said. "Perhaps wait until you've eaten them before passing judgement."

The men all sat at the table and stared at her. Despite being hardened cowboys, Emma noticed that each one of them was waiting for her to eat before they did. It made her believe they'd been told to be on their best behavior.

She lifted her knife and fork and took a mouthful. Not meaning to sound vain, she decided it was good. Emma closed her eyes and savored every flavor that had soothed her taste buds. The fact she had eaten little for days probably helped.

The low groans around the table worried her. "Is it that bad? I'm sorry," she said, fighting back tears. She doubted Marcus would let her stay after all. If she couldn't make a decent pancake, what else would she mess up?

It had to be nerves. And lack of sleep. Normally, her cooking was more than acceptable. Emma was convinced that they would show her the door. Hopefully not until the morning.

"Bad?" Marcus said, turning to face her. "This is the best food we've eaten for a long time. Isn't that right?" he asked the others around the table.

They all nodded and filled their mouths again. Emma breathed a sigh of relief.

When everyone had finished eating, Emma collected up the soiled dishes.

"Thank you for a wonderful meal," Buck said as he stood. He appeared to be the oldest of the cowboys. The man's face seemed far more weathered than the others. It was obvious to Emma he'd been around for a while.

The other men followed his lead.

It was soon apparent what was going on. Emma put her hands on her hips. "Sit down. Now," she demanded. "What sort of cook would I be if I didn't dish up a heartwarming dessert?" As the men took their places once more, Emma took two apple pies from the oven and cut them into slices and dished them up. "Help yourselves," she said, as she prepared coffee for each man.

Emma placed a large bowl of clotted cream in the center of the table, and she took great joy in watching each man eat and enjoy her creations.

Sitting back at the table, Emma took in the scene around the table. All five cowboys looked far happier than when they arrived. Good food in their bellies seemed to do that, and it made Emma feel good inside.

Having good food to eat made her feel better, too. Having left in such a hurry meant she'd fled with little, and that included money. All Emma had with her at the time was her reticule. She never carried a lot of cash, which was usually the safest way to go. This time, it was to her detriment.

"Thank you, Miss Seymour," Gus said, ushering the other cowboys out the door.

Marcus lingered behind. "The fire needs stoking," he said, and hurried across to the fireplace. Situated between the sitting room and the kitchen, the warmth spread to where it was needed the most. He pushed the embers around, then threw more logs on the fire. Emma could picture herself huddled under a blanket, taking in the warmth of a burning fire on these cold winter nights.

Except she wouldn't be here beyond tomorrow. Where she would go, and how she would get there, Emma did not know. The little money she had paid for her stagecoach ticket, with a small amount left over. She'd used that money to purchase scant food during the trip. She'd had to make do with an apple and a sandwich over her days of travel. It was devastating to think she had money in her bank account but couldn't access it for fear Sheriff Tommy Yates would find out where she was.

After washing the dishes and cleaning the kitchen, Emma wandered over to the sitting room, lapping up the warmth of the fire. The question of her status at the ranch was on her lips, but Emma didn't know what to say. Would Marcus let her stay as his housekeeper, or would he send her away? The latter seemed more likely since, according to his conversation with Gus, he'd resisted for a long time already.

"Supper was wonderful," he told her as he continued to squat in front of the fire, which was now burning well. "I could easily get used to it." He glanced over his shoulder at her. "I know the other men could, too." He smiled then, and a shiver of anticipation shot down Emma's spine. Did that mean…? She shook herself mentally. She was reading far too much into his words.

She sat in a chair close to the fire. Then abruptly stood. "Is this your chair?" she asked abruptly as she fidgeted with her hands.

He stood then, apparently happy with the burning logs that gave so much warmth to the room. "You can sit there," he told her. "There are plenty of other chairs."

Emma took that as meaning it was his favorite chair. He was willing to give it up for her. His actions confused her. Why would he do that, except perhaps he was being polite? Marcus watched her carefully as she took the few steps to the chair opposite. She cringed as he chuckled, but sat down anyway.

Marcus sat on the chair Emma had vacated, then leaned forward. Suddenly the smile was gone, and so was the casual air he'd had only moments before. "What are your plans?" he asked gently.

"I…I have no plans," she answered, her voice low. Emma stared down into her hands as they sat entwined on her lap. "I have no money, so no means of leaving. Besides, where would I go?" She blinked several times, trying to hold back her tears. Marcus stared at her for what seemed like forever.

He stood and walked over to the fire. Whether that was to get away from her physically, or because he was nervous, Emma didn't know. As he stared down at the flames, he picked up the poker and again stoked the fire. Not that it was needed.

Unexpectedly, he turned around and glanced down at her. "I've been told I can't have you staying here without a chaperone. Apparently, it will ruin your reputation."

Emma's heart thudded. He was kicking her out. Right now, apparently. In the cold and the dark, amidst the snow that continued to fall. She had no hope of stopping her tears now. They flooded her cheeks, and he came over to her, squatting once more, only this time, he rubbed a hand over her back.

"I didn't mean…" Marcus ran a hand through his hair. "I'm bad at this sort of thing," he added. "It's been suggested we get married." He grimaced then, and Emma knew he was asking her under duress. "What do you think?"

It was a lot to take in, and Emma took a long, fortifying breath. Marrying would mean her name would change, which would protect her from Tommy. She closed her eyes to think through the possibilities and outcomes.

When she opened her eyes again, he was staring at her. Emma opened her mouth to speak, but he beat her to it.

"I'm not thrilled about it either, but it will keep your reputation intact. We can go to town in the morning. I'm sure the preacher can fit us in."

"Is…is this to be a temporary situation?" she asked. Not that she expected she would ever be safe again. Not while Tommy was alive and free. Which meant she would never be safe.

"A marriage of convenience would work best," he said, his words firm. Emma noticed his eyes searched the room. Not once had he looked at her since putting forward his proposal. If you could call it that.

"I need to give it some thought," she said. The moment the words were out of her mouth, Emma knew she'd been impulsive. What choice did she have? Marcus was right – she was a single woman staying alone with a single man.

"You said you were in a difficult situation," Marcus said. His expression told her a lot. He was running out of patience with her, and that wasn't what she'd hoped for.

Her heart rate increased, and Emma felt light-headed. Too much had happened in the last week. Life-changing events that led her here. "You're right," she whispered, then turned away to hide her errant tears.

Was she so repulsive that Marcus didn't want her as a proper wife? Was that her life once she married him – a life of loneliness, living with a man who despised her? No wonder her tears fell hot and fast.

Chapter Four

Marcus couldn't believe his ears. Emma refused his offer – the one Gus told him he should make. Buck made his opinion known as well. As the oldest of the cowboys, he'd been around a long time, and he'd seen a lot.

Marcus trusted both men's opinions. Strangely, Emma was crying, and he couldn't fathom why. Was it because he put it forward more like a business proposal than a marriage one? He mentally slapped himself.

Trust him to put his foot in it. But now he had to try and make things right. "None of that came out the way I meant it," Marcus said.

Emma swiped a hand across her face, then turned to face him. He'd have to be a fool not to notice her red eyes. It was all he could do not to go to Emma's side and pull her into his arms. "Forget about it," she whispered. "I'm not the marrying kind. Besides, you don't want to get mixed up with the likes of me."

She turned away again, leaving Marcus to wonder what she meant by that. His mind went back to an earlier conversation they'd had. What was it she'd said? *I had to flee for my life.* Surely she was exaggerating.

"If you agree, we'll go to town in the morning and visit the preacher. Then we'll go to the mercantile and get you some clothes and whatever else you need."

Her back stiffened. "I have my own money," she said firmly. Then her face seemed to tense. "Except I can't access it or he'll know where I am," she whispered, her voice emotional. Her eyes darted all around the room. They glanced everywhere except at him.

Marcus was starting to get a picture of why Emma had hidden in his loft. It could take forever to get all the details out of her, but the story was beginning to unravel.

Dare he ask for the full story? It was obvious something terrible had happened. That someone, clearly a man, was trying to find her, but why? "We need to talk," he said firmly but quietly. "If we are to marry, I need to know what I'm getting into."

Emma stared at him, her face devoid of color. After what seemed forever, she shook her head. "The less you know, the better."

Marcus didn't agree, but he couldn't force her to tell him everything. She would tell him in her own time. "Are my men in danger?" he asked, when the thought came into his mind.

"I…I honestly don't know. He's ruthless, I can tell you that much."

Emma's words hit him hard. Marcus was more convinced than ever that he needed to know what they were up against. "Miss Seymour, Emma," he said gently. "Tell me what's going on. I can't have you staying here unless you tell me the full story." He leaned back to let his words sink in.

You could have heard a pin drop in the silence that followed. Then suddenly she jumped up out of the chair and glanced at him. "I'm tired," she said. "I will see you in the morning."

Emma then hurried to the room he'd allocated as her bedroom, leaving Marcus to ponder what on earth she'd got involved in.

~*~

Marcus awoke to the sound of clattering in the kitchen. It was a rare sound in his home, and it had him on alert.

Until he remembered Emma Seymour was staying here. Most likely, it was her puttering about. A smile came to his face at the thought of what she was making for breakfast. This morning, he would again press her for information about the man who was pursuing her. He totally understood she was afraid, but he needed to know exactly what he could be dealing with.

In a matter of hours, they would be married. She would be his responsibility for the rest of their days. It would be up to him to protect her, but how did he do so if she refused to disclose any information?

He needed to think straight, so quickly dressed and headed to the bathroom. Splashing cold water on his face helped Marcus to wake up. Did he really want to marry this stranger? Perhaps they should put it off for a day or two.

On the other hand, if they waited too long, the roads would be difficult to navigate with the snow covering them.

Marcus strode into the kitchen, feeling far more awake because of the freezing water. "Good morning," he said. Emma jumped. "I apologize. I didn't mean to startle you," he said, feeling more than a little guilty at startling her.

She nodded, but didn't utter a word. Emma had her hand to her chest, and Marcus was certain her heart was pounding from the fright he'd given her. He stepped closer and led her to sit down at the kitchen table. They sat there in silence. "I really am sorry," he said gently. "Would a mug of tea help?" He shook himself mentally. What a stupid thing to say.

Emma's eyes burned him. Was she assessing what sort of fool he was? That was exactly how he felt – that he'd made a fool of himself.

"That would be nice," she finally said, then put her head to the table as though she lacked sleep.

"Did you sleep well?" he asked as he poured tea for Emma and coffee for himself. She lifted her head from the table and glanced at him.

"Not at all," she said. "Apart from being pursued by a madman, I've now put you and your men in danger." Tears welled up in her eyes, but she blinked them away.

Marcus placed the tea in front of her and sat next to Emma. He covered her hand with his own. She said nothing, but her eyes burned into their entwined hands. Trying to comfort her was not working, so he pulled his hand away. "Tell me about this man. Why is he after you?"

Emma closed her eyes and took a deep breath, letting it out slowly. "I inadvertently witnessed him kill four men." Her eyes filled with tears again. This time, they escaped and slid down her face.

"Did you go to the sheriff?" he asked gently. That would be the first thing she should have done.

She closed her eyes again momentarily, then stared at him. "He *is* the sheriff," she whispered.

Chapter Five

Emma knew she would never forget the shocked expression on Marcus's face when she'd told him the truth. If ever there was a time for him to back out of their agreement to marry, it was now. Her heart pounded. What if he changed his mind? With no money to her name, and no worldly possessions, she would be in a desperate situation. She was effectively destitute.

Although she had at first been taken aback by his proposal of marriage, Emma knew it was the only way out of her predicament. Not only would it give her a safe place to live, her soon-to-be husband would protect her.

That is, unless he changed his mind.

"The sheriff, you say?" He shook his head in disbelief. "What sort of sheriff is he?"

The question was rhetorical, and Emma knew it. Still, she answered. "Tommy Yates is as evil as they come. It's not the first time he's killed for no good reason. Even as a young boy, the signs were there."

A shudder wracked her body. Why the town's people hadn't done something about Tommy all those years ago, she would never know. Except she did – his father was the previous sheriff, and ignored all the signs. It was rather ironic that Tommy would kill his father to secure his position as sheriff. Of course, his death was passed off as a tragic accident.

Tommy seemed to have a knack for getting away with his murderous sprees.

Emma shuddered again. The more she thought about him, the more terrified she became. Marriage was one of the few things that would save her. If he couldn't find her, he couldn't kill her. Knowing him the way she did, Emma knew Tommy eventually would find a way.

With her being on Marcus's ranch, she was putting everyone else in danger. It was an unacceptable risk. "I...I can't marry you," she whispered, her eyes searching his reaction. "It's far too dangerous for you and your men." The emotion in her voice gave her away. She was terrified, but also knew this was her only chance of getting away from the man who wanted her dead.

Marcus reached across and held both her hands. He caressed the back of her hand with his thumb. It was as though he didn't realize what he was doing. Emma wasn't sure that was a good thing. Especially if they were to have a marriage of convenience. "We will protect you," Marcus said firmly, then reached for his mug of coffee. "The men will be in for breakfast soon. We'll work it out, I promise you. You will be safe here."

There was nothing she could do but nod. Emma gulped down the last of her tea, then stood, ready to prepare breakfast. "Are we still going to see the preacher?" Marcus asked, his words cautious.

She stared at him. What choice did she have? Marcus was right when he said she'd be safe on his ranch. At least she hoped that would be the case. On the bright side, he was a strong and handsome man. Despite the short time they'd known each other, he seemed to care about her. That had to be a bonus, surely?

Or perhaps all he was interested in was her cooking and housekeeping skills. Emma knew she would probably never know.

Moments later, the men descended into the kitchen. Emma made coffee for each of them and apologized for the delay with their meal. None seemed worried.

She'd already collected eggs from the henhouse and had prepared the bacon ready to cook. Before Marcus had risen, she'd made the toast and placed it in the oven to keep hot. The banter coming from the table warmed her heart, and Emma knew she was exactly where she was meant to be.

Still, it didn't lessen her worry about the danger they may end up facing.

The moment the food was ready, she dished up the meals and handed them out. Once each man had a plate of food in front of him, she added the toast to the center of the table. Then she sat down and joined them.

Emma glanced around the table. These were all good men. She hadn't known them long, but it was easy to see the goodness that surrounded them. How could she put their lives in danger? It wasn't fair. "I need to tell you something," she said to no one in particular. Each man put his cutlery down. Until that moment, they'd been happily eating the food she'd prepared for them.

Marcus reached across and put his hand to her arm in an effort to stop her. "Not now," he told the cowboys. "After breakfast." They all focused on Marcus. At least now they weren't staring at her.

Emma turned to face him. "I'm sorry," she whispered.

"Let them eat, and we'll talk then." He removed his hand, and Emma wished it back. It was crazy. She'd known Marcus Tyler for a little more than sixteen hours. Yet his touch sent shivers down her spine. When he held her, she felt comforted and reassured. He wanted a marriage of convenience. She wanted more.

"This is good," Buck said. "I've lived on this ranch for most of my adult life," he said. "Over twenty years. Never has the food been so good." He shoved another mouthful of food into his mouth and seemed to savor the taste. "Girly, we are happy to have you as part of our family."

The other men muttered their agreement, then went back to their meal.

A tear slipped down Emma's cheek, and Marcus brushed it away. "We're a family here," he told her. "Everything will work out."

Buck stared at both her and Marcus. He opened his mouth to speak, but Marcus shook his head. "All in good time, Buck," he said gently. It was enough for the older man to go back to his food, despite the frown on his face.

Emma picked at her food. Despite Marcus's best intentions, if these men weren't prepared to look out for her, she may need to move on again. She still had her stagecoach ticket. Since she did not know where she would end up, she'd bought a ticket that allowed her to go anywhere. If this didn't work out, she would ask Marcus to take her to town, and take the next stagecoach to goodness knew where. It would break her heart, but she had to do what would give here the best chance of survival.

It was a hard lesson to learn, but Emma had to make herself the priority.

Emma cleared the table and began to wash the dishes. Marcus ushered the men into the sitting room. That way, they could talk openly and not worry about Emma overhearing them. She could hear low mutterings, but couldn't make out the words. At this very moment, her life was in their hands. The four men who worked for Marcus would decide her next steps. If they refused to protect her, there was nothing to be done except leave.

Marcus told Emma he didn't believe it would be the case, but she had her doubts. If she was forced to leave Marcus's Mountain View Ranch, she didn't know where she would go. She couldn't continue to take the stagecoach for much longer. It was backbreaking being in a stagecoach for long hours. Let alone the worry of who you were traveling with. Besides, she could not access her bank account for fear Tommy would locate her. She was in an unenviable position.

Emma finished drying the dishes, then placed them back in the cupboard where they belonged. When she turned back around, five men stood in front of her. Emma hadn't heard them arrive - likely because she was preoccupied with her troubles.

Buck stepped forward. "I'm sorry to hear about your situation," he said. "We are all in agreement." He stepped closer, then hugged her. "We are all happy to protect you," he said, then stepped back. Each man took a turn at hugging her, ending with

Marcus. He lingered far longer, and his hug was the one that really mattered to her.

"Thank you," she said, the emotion in her voice hard to miss. "I appreciate every one of you."

"We appreciate you and your cooking skills," Buck said. "I mean…not only because of your cooking."

The others laughed, and they all left without another word. Except Marcus. "Let me know when you're ready and we'll head into town."

It was really happening. Emma had agreed to marry a man she'd known for a disturbingly short time. It was almost like becoming a mail-order bride, except she had met Marcus. From what she'd seen so far, he was a good, respectable man.. He could have handed her over to the sheriff the moment he'd discovered her up in his loft. Or worse still, could have taken liberties.

Except he didn't. Instead, he'd taken her under his wing, and gave her a chance to explain. For that, Emma was truly grateful. "Are you certain you still want to do this? Especially now you're aware of the circumstances." She hoped and prayed Marcus hadn't changed his mind, but she had to give him the opportunity to back out.

He stared down into her face. "I know what I'm doing," he said as he pulled her into his arms. Emma relaxed against his chest. She shouldn't – that wasn't the agreement. Marcus wanted a marriage of convenience. She would be his cook and housekeeper, and he would protect her.

It was as simple as that. Or was it?

Chapter Six

They drove into town in near silence. Marcus pulled the blanket up over Emma's lap further. She seemed oblivious to the cold and the snow. She had other things on her mind, he was certain. Like marrying a complete stranger to keep safe.

Knowing what he knew now, he didn't blame her. Marcus was glad it was his wagon she'd climbed into that day. What if it had belonged to someone sinister? There were a few men who came to mind who would not have treated her with the respect she deserved.

It pained him to think that way, but Marcus knew it was true. He glanced across at the woman sitting beside him and wondered what was going through her mind. At least today, they could use the buggy. It kept most of the snow off them, which helped a lot with the cold. He couldn't imagine what Emma had gone through hiding in the back of his wagon. It would not be the most comfortable of rides.

Still, she'd got through it. That alone proved to Marcus she was tough. Witnessing not one but four murders would have been horrific. Marcus vowed to ensure the so-called sheriff of Blacktown answered for his actions, even if it was the last thing he did.

He turned back to face the road. The snow could be treacherous. Thankfully, it wasn't as heavy as it would get closer to Christmas. Despite that, it was bitterly cold. He had to make sure Emma was appropriately outfitted before they left town. She would need a full wardrobe, including a thick coat, gloves and scarf. She had none of those.

The connection he'd felt for her right from the start had not wavered. What drew him to her, Marcus wasn't sure. Finding her asleep in the loft, on a bale of hay, tugged at his heart from the moment he'd found her. It was clear even then, she was in a spot of trouble. How much trouble had soon become apparent. "We're almost there," he said louder than he'd planned. His voice seemed to startle her. Had she drifted off to sleep? He could only imagine how little sleep she'd had over the past days. His heart broke for her.

"That's good," Emma told him, then hooked her arm through his. "It is bitterly cold. I can't wait to get inside and out of the cold."

He had given her his spare coat to wear. There was no way her thin cotton gown would keep the cold away. It may not pass as a woman's coat, or be the most fashionable piece, but he had no intention of letting her leave the ranch without suitable attire. She'd balked at the thought of wearing a coat meant for a man, but he was certain she would be grateful for the added warmth the garment provided.

She rested her head on his shoulder as though it were the most natural thing in the world. Warmth flooded Marcus, despite the cold and the snow. That she felt comfortable enough with him to do so made him happy. His hope was they had a good marriage, even if it was one of convenience.

His thoughts gave Marcus pause. Why had he even suggested such a thing? Emma was a beautiful woman, and already he had feelings for her. But he'd made the declaration, and he had to stick by it.

His heart pounded as they pulled up outside the church. It was already too late to take it back. A marriage of convenience, it was.

The ceremony took less than fifteen minutes. Marcus saw the disappointment on Emma's face, but there was nothing he could do about it. As a young girl, she probably dreamed of a big wedding, with all the pomp and ceremony that went with it. No doubt, a church filled with friends and family was part of the dream. Instead, she had the organist and the preacher's wife, who acted as witnesses.

He felt bad for her, but there was nothing he could do about it. "We'll go to the mercantile first, then have lunch at the diner before returning to the ranch."

"Oh, lunch!" Emma exclaimed. "I need to be home to make lunch."

Marcus liked that she already thought of the Mountain View Ranch as home. "I told the men we would be gone much of the day. They'll do what they did every day before you arrived – they will make their own lunch."

As they stood outside the church, Emma glanced about. She likely didn't get to see much of the town when she arrived. It was probably a case of leave the stagecoach as quickly as it arrived, then once she'd located his wagon, climb in it and keep quiet. She certainly did a good job of that.

"That's the mercantile over there," Marcus said, pointing in the right direction. "And next door is the bakery. We also have a bootmaker, barber, and a dressmaker. The saloon is a recent addition to the town, unfortunately," he said, as he grimaced. "We could well do without it. Over there is the diner."

Guiding Emma to the mercantile, he felt somehow different. Marcus didn't understand it, but knew it had something to do with his marriage only minutes ago. With marriage came more responsibility. He thought of himself as already being responsible, but now he had Emma to care for as well. Protecting her would likely be a big part of that. He reached forward and opened the door to the mercantile, ushering Emma ahead of himself.

"Mornin' Marcus." The words came before he even spotted Howard Janson, the mercantile owner. "Who's the pretty lady?" Howard looked Emma up and down, but Marcus knew he meant nothing by it. Howard liked to know who was frequenting his store.

He guided Emma to the front counter. "This is Emma, my wife," he said, warmth filling him at the thought.

"Wife!" Howard was more than a little surprised, and Marcus wasn't in the least surprised. He'd been a confirmed bachelor for all his adult life. "Welcome, Mrs. Tyler. It's very nice to meet you. This is my wife Miriam," he said as she came to stand by her husband.

Miriam smiled. "Congratulations to you both," she said, and Marcus knew she would be genuinely happy for them. She then addressed Marcus. "Didn't you tell me marriage was never an option for you?" She grinned then, and Marcus knew he had to think quickly.

"A man can change his mind, can't he?" He knew that answer wouldn't appease either of them. "I'm pushing forty. If I didn't marry soon, there would be no chance of heirs," he said. It was a lie, and he knew it was. There would be no heirs for him, since he'd vowed they would not even sleep together.

Emma studied him. She knew he was lying, but he had to say something that could be even remotely true. Otherwise... He shook himself mentally. Enough had been said. "We're looking for clothes for Emma. She has no clothes," he began, then realized he'd have to explain why.

"Stage people lost your trunk, did they?" Miriam asked. "They have a habit of doing that. Follow me, and we'll get you sorted." She stared down at the drab coat Marcus had loaned his wife, and helped her out of it, handing it to its proper owner.

It was all Marcus could do to withhold a sigh of relief. If Miriam wanted to believe that Emma's clothes were lost in transit, so be it. He had no intention of putting her right.

It seemed like forever before the two women emerged from the back of the store, but Miriam held a box full of gowns, scarves, gloves, nightgowns, a warm coat, and he hoped, whatever number of unmentionables she required. The pair headed toward the front counter. "It's too much," Emma protested.

"It's really not, Marcus," Miriam said firmly. "With no clothing whatsoever to her name, Emma needs the basics, and that's what she's got."

"Put it all on my account, and anything else you believe she needs."

Emma came to stand beside her husband. "It's definitely too much," she whispered.

He gazed down into her concerned face. "It really isn't," Marcus said, then planted a kiss on her forehead. "You need clothes, and besides, I want to spoil you. It's that simple." He pulled her close and wrapped an arm around her back. Marcus was breaking his own rule. Keeping his distance was the only way to keep their marriage loveless. As much as he had feelings for Emma, there would come a day when she no longer needed protecting. Who was to say she wouldn't decide to leave?

He wasn't willing to risk it.

Chapter Seven

Emma knew Marcus meant well, but she cringed at how much her new clothes cost. Not that he seemed worried, but she did. "I have some money," she protested, but once again, he calmed her fears, pulling her closer still.

He helped Emma into her new woolen coat, then turned to the storekeepers. "We'll come back to collect our purchases after we've eaten," Marcus told Miriam firmly. In other words, he was disregarding any objections Emma had to his spending spree.

The best thing she could do was to leave now. She'd already cost her new husband a fortune, and they'd been married for less than an hour. Her heart was pounding. Instead of feeling relieved about marrying Marcus, she felt far worse. She didn't want him to spend his hard earned money on her. To keep up her end of the bargain, Emma was to cook and clean for him, and Marcus would protect her in return.

There was nothing in their agreement that said he would replenish her wardrobe and spoil her in the process. As they left the mercantile, cold air hit her right in the face. Emma felt better about being seen in public because she was now wearing the new coat, scarf, and gloves Marcus had purchased for her. She could have changed into one of her new gowns, but Emma refused the offer. She was certain Marcus would be eager to get back to the ranch, and didn't want to hold him up further.

"You look real pretty in that red coat," he said. "The color suits you." Marcus's words sent a shiver down her spine.

He hooked her arm through his and guided Emma toward the diner. "You should enjoy the food here. They serve good, home-cooked meals."

As soon as they set foot on the boardwalk outside the diner, the door flew open and they were guided inside. "Marcus, this is a surprise."

"A good one, I hope." He grinned, and warmth flooded Emma. Marcus rarely smiled, but when he did, it lit up his entire face. "Grace, this is my wife, Emma."

The expression on the other woman's face showed she was clearly shocked. "Wife? You're married?" At first, Emma believed Grace was jealous, but the thought soon left her. "How wonderful for you both. It is way pastime you found a good woman." She stepped in and embraced Emma and then Marcus.

After studying them for a moment, Grace guided them to a table near the back. That suited Emma just fine. It was far better than a window table that left them wide open for attack. Not that she expected Tommy Yates to have located her – yet, even so, caution was necessary in her situation.

After handing each of them a menu, Grace disappeared into the kitchen. She reappeared a short time later with a jug of water and two glasses. She poured a glass of water for each of them. "Our special today is chicken pot pie," she said. "The desert special is cherry cobbler. Would you like me to come back while you decide?" She glanced from one to the other of them.

"Chicken pot pie sounds perfect for me," Emma said fully anticipating the meal. "No dessert though."

Marcus studied her. "I'll have the steak and veg, thanks Grace. We'll also have two cherry cobblers. This is our wedding celebration meal. Nothing but the best."

Now the other woman appeared stunned. "When did you get married, if it's not too much to ask?"

Marcus grinned again. When he did that, Emma's heart fluttered. She wished it wouldn't, because she couldn't afford to get close to a man who was not interested in a true relationship with her. "This morning," he said, and reached across the table to hold Emma's hand.

"That's wonderful," Grace said, then disappeared into the kitchen again.

Emma felt there was something between these two, perhaps in the past, but Grace seemed visibly shocked to hear of Marcus's marriage. It was fleeting, but disappointment crossed her face more than once. "The two of you were more than friends," she stated blandly. Was she a little jealous? She hoped not.

Marcus frowned. "That is very perceptive of you. We dated many years ago, but it didn't work out. We've stayed friends though."

So there she had it. Emma was right after all.

It wasn't long before their food arrived, and they ate their meal in silence. Emma hated keeping Marcus from his work. She had learned he only came into town once a month to restore supplies. He had done that already this month, which was when she stowed away on his wagon. Because of her, he'd returned again today, but this time to marry her. He'd done that out of pity for Emma, and she hated that he felt obligated to do so.

They'd not long finished eating when Grace came to collect their soiled dishes. "Coffee for you,

Marcus? What about you, Emma? What do you drink?"

"I prefer tea," Emma said, and Marcus confirmed he'd have the coffee. The next time Grace appeared it was with both the beverages, as well as their desserts.

"This is good," Emma said. She was glad Marcus had insisted she have dessert. "I know it's probably too soon, but what do you do on the ranch for Christmas?" Having never lived on a ranch, she didn't know if the cowboys stayed, or went home to family.

Marcus studied her. "When we had a cook, which was a few years ago now, he made a roast for Christmas dinner. With no cook, we've had to make do."

Emma nodded, but knew she would make Christmas dinner special this year. "Do you mind telling me why your cook left?" Hopefully, she wasn't overstepping the mark.

Marcus seemed astonished at her question. His eyes had opened wide, then he studied her again. "I should have told you," he said quietly. "Cookie didn't leave. He died of consumption," Marcus said, his expression now one of sadness.

Reaching across the table, Emma covered his hands. "I'm sorry," she said softly. "I shouldn't have asked.

Shaking his head, Marcus refuted her words. "I should have told you. It was a blow for everyone on the ranch. We all loved Cookie." Marcus took a long sip of his coffee.

It was clear to Emma he was still grieving over the loss. Not that she could do anything about it, except do her best to take over where their beloved cook left off. "No wonder you all love my cooking. What have you been eating – sausages and beans?" She wouldn't put it past them. Emma had heard stories about the poor eating habits of cowboys. "That changes now," she said, and stared at Marcus until he squirmed under her intense gaze.

"No," he said, sounding wounded. "We had stew, bacon and eggs, and sausages. Sometimes with potatoes and onions. I can't think of the other food we had."

It made Emma wonder if she needed to get even more supplies from the mercantile. She decided to wait and see for herself. She knew what was in the pantry, but what the root cellar held, she had no idea. She hadn't ventured that far. If she needed to come to town again, surely someone at the ranch could bring her.

"We should visit the sheriff's office before we leave town," Marcus said firmly. In other words, he wasn't giving her a choice.

They wandered down to see the sheriff, the entire time, Emma was filled with dread. Would the sheriff laugh in her face? Tommy Yates was a colleague to him – how would he take to the accusations she was about to make?

Marcus opened the door, and stood aside to let her go ahead. Emma would have run in the opposite direction if Marcus hadn't been there to stop her.

Chapter Eight

Marcus could see at a glance Emma was terrified, and quickly closed the door behind them. Sheriff Holt Garrett was a good man. He'd been sheriff of Mountain View for as long as Marcus could remember. He wasn't young, but neither was he old.

The sheriff leaned back in his chair. Emma didn't take her eyes off him for even one second. She held tightly to Marcus's hand, and he wasn't complaining, despite knowing he should.

Without warning, Holt began to shuffle papers around on his desk. It confused Marcus. So far he hadn't taken any notes, but it was clear the sheriff was concerned.

"Is this the man?" he asked, holding up a wanted poster.

Emma gasped, and her already pale face became ashen. She nodded, then answered so quietly, her voice was barely audible. "That's him. I…I don't understand," she said, her confusion clear.

"You weren't the only one to witness his murderous spree. Not to mention the marshals have been following his dirty deeds for a while. They knew what was going on but had no proof."

"And now they do," Marcus interjected, his heart pounding. What did that mean for Emma?

"As it happens," Sheriff Garrett said, "two marshals are here in town right now. They're passing through, but informed me about the Tommy Yates situation."

"What now?" Marcus asked, although he was certain he already knew the answer.

"Keep your wife safe. She needs protection." The sheriff squirmed and Marcus couldn't work out why.

He studied the other man. "Is he…?" Marcus let the sentence hang, not wanting to say too much. The last thing he wanted to do was frighten Emma even more.

"He is," Sheriff Garrett said. "Yates is in the wind." He let out a huge sigh, and Marcus was certain it was from frustration.

Emma glanced up at Marcus. He could see she was confused. "In the wind?" she asked.

Sherrif Garrett stood. "We don't know where he is," the sheriff explained. "Which means you, my dear, need to stay out of sight."

Marcus was certain Emma would break down in tears. Instead she stood and shook the sheriff's hand. "Thank you for your candor, Sheriff. I appreciate it," she said, then headed for the door.

"Emma, wait," Marcus called. "You need to stay with me. We don't know what we're dealing with." She nodded, but Marcus worried she may still go ahead without him.

"I will speak with the marshals before they leave town. I'll see if we can get their assistance in this matter."

Marcus shook the sheriff's hand and thanked him for his help. He had his eyes on the sheriff, while trying to watch Emma. It was an impossible task. In the end, he knew which one was more important, and went after his wife.

Already, he knew protecting his new wife would be a difficult task. She was determined to keep things normal, despite having a target on her back.

"Are you ready to leave?" Marcus asked as they headed back to the wagon. "It's a long drive home."

Taking a deep breath, Emma seemed to be preparing herself for further bad news. He waited as she slowly let it out again. Stepping closer, he put his arm around her shoulders. "It will be alright," he said. "I promise."

She glanced at him and frowned. "You can't know that," she whispered. Not that anyone was nearby to hear, but from what he'd seen, Emma dropped her voice when she was scared or worried. He didn't blame her.

"We have four good men back at the ranch. They all adore you, and want to protect you." As I do, he wanted to add, but thought the better of it, not wanting to bare his feelings to this stranger, who was now his wife.

Instead they went back to the buggy, where he held Emma by the waist as she climbed up. "I can do it myself," she said crossly. "How do you think I hid in your wagon?"

He removed his hands and threw them up in the air. He decided this was her way of letting off steam. It had been a difficult day for Emma, and she had every right to be angry. He just happened to be the one who was closest to her. As he stepped back to give her room, she stumbled. Had he been a lesser man, Marcus would have let her fall.

Except he wasn't like that. He cared for Emma. Far too much. As he reached out and held her close, he noticed the shine to her eyes. She might want him to think she was this brave woman who needed nobody's help, but he knew better. "It's fine to accept help," he said tenderly, his arms still around her. Marcus gently put her to the ground, and Emma closed her eyes and shook her head. The movement was barely visible, but it was there. They stood like that for several minutes. He let her contemplate the new information Sheriff Garrett had shared. It would not have been easy to digest, knowing Tommy Yates was on the run and could be coming for her.

"You're right," she said quietly, after having a chance to calm down. "I do need your help. I apologize for being so abrupt before. It was rude of me, to say the least." Tears hovered on the ends of her eyelashes, and Marcus could see how close she was to breaking down. He understood her frustration, and felt the same way.

It seemed like no one was doing anything to keep her safe. Except it wasn't true. Marcus and his men would protect her day and night. They had already made a roster. At no time would Emma be alone and unprotected.

~*~

They'd only been in the buggy for mere moments when Sheriff Garrett came running toward them. "Would you come back to my office?" he asked, studying Emma. "The marshals are there and would like to talk to you, Mrs. Tyler."

"It's Emma," she told him, and before Marcus could answer, she was already climbing to the ground.

Reaching out to her once he had alighted, Marcus went to her side. "I'm right here with you," he said softly, and they strode back to the sheriff's office.

They may not have known each other long, but he could tell she was withdrawn. Emma's ordeal was all too much for her. If he could, he'd pack up and leave, taking her far from all her troubles. Unfortunately, it was not possible, nor was it feasible. He had responsibilities at the ranch, and needed to ensure not only Emma was safe, but also his men.

As they walked back to the sheriff's office, Marcus could feel Emma shaking. He pulled her a little closer. "It will be fine," he told her, despite knowing that may not be the truth. One thing he knew was he would protect her with his life.

Chapter Nine

Emma's heart hammered as they headed back to the sheriff's office. The first time there was bad enough, but now she had to face two marshals as well.

"Mrs. Tyler," Sheriff Garrett said, and pulled out a chair for her. He indicated for Marcus to sit as well, which made her feel a little better. Emma knew she couldn't face this alone. "Let me introduce Marshal Gregson and Marshal Holmes. They would like to talk about your encounter with Tommy Yates." The sheriff stepped back, and the two marshals stepped closer.

"I'm Marshal Peter Holmes," one of the marshals said. "I need to know exactly what you saw, and what happened next." He sat down at the sheriff's desk, his pencil poised to take notes.

Emma took a fortifying breath, then let it out slowly. Marcus squeezed her hand, giving Emma the support she needed. "I was minding my own business, strolling along the walkway, heading toward the mercantile. As I turned the corner, I glanced down into the alleyway. Four men were running, and Sheriff Tommy Yates shot each man in the back. One. After. The. Other." The memory of that day flashed back in her mind. It was far too vivid and Emma wanted to forget it ever happened. Sadly, she knew it would never leave her.

A shiver went down her spine, and tears sprang to her eyes. Emma swiped at them, and with Marcus continuing to hold her hand firmly gave her the courage to go on. "I must have made a sound, a gasp or maybe I screamed. I don't recall, but Tommy turned around and stared at me. He didn't say a word, but I knew if I stayed in town, I would be next." Her entire body shuddered, and she wanted to flee, but Emma knew she must stay.

"He didn't threaten you?" Marshal Holmes asked, curiosity on his face.

Emma shook her head. "He didn't have to. Everyone who knew Tommy well, knew he was dangerous. He only had to give you that evil stare of his, and that was enough to keep people quiet."

Marshal Gregson stepped closer. "We know he's done this before. What we need know is enough information to build a strong case against him." He turned to face the other marshal, but only momentarily. "You are our star witness. We have another witness to a previous murder, and that person has already given a statement. Except now he's disappeared."

Emma gasped. Did that mean Tommy had silenced the other person? Her heart hammered so badly, she was certain she would pass out. Emma stood, and turned to leave. She could hear murmurs in the background, including Marcus asking if she was alright.

She was far from alright, and Emma knew it. She shook her head, and that was when she collapsed to the floor.

~*~

When she awoke, Emma glanced up to find Marcus standing over her, along with a man she'd never seen before.

"Ah, she's awake. As I said earlier, Marcus, it's shock." The doctor reached out a hand, and helped Emma to sit up. "How are you feeling now?" he asked. "You might still be a little lightheaded."

"Just a little," Emma said. At almost the same time she realized where she was. Someone, most likely Marcus, had picked her up and carried her into a jail cell. "Why am I here?" she asked Marcus.

He shrugged. "It's better than the wooden floor," he answered. He was probably right. At least she wasn't being treated like a criminal, which was her first thought.

The three lawman pushed their way into the tiny jail cell. "You three, get out!" the doctor demanded.

"Mrs. Tyler had this turn because of you. I am demanding you leave her alone."

Marcus stared at the doctor momentarily, then spoke. "I'm with the doc. I'm taking my wife home. I don't want you badgering her again."

As much as she was relieved, Emma wondered how safe it would be for not only herself, but Marcus and his workers. "It's not safe with me there. I'm sorry, Marcus, but I must leave town." It pained her to say the words, but she'd already grown fond of her new husband and his cowpokes. She refused to be responsible for them being injured or even killed by Tommy Yates.

The sheriff turned to the marshals. "We need to talk," he told them, and the three men left. Emma could hear them talking, but couldn't make out the words.

"I can't let you leave town," Marcus said firmly. "You are my wife, and I will protect you."

Emma knew Marcus was trying to do what he believed was right, but Emma knew it wasn't for the best. "We can get an annulment. We've only been married for a few hours."

Marcus shook his head. She could see his frustration but there was nothing she could do about it. "I refuse to agree to an annulment, which means it won't happen." He stood up then, and stormed out of the jail cell.

Perhaps he was letting her go after all?

It wasn't long before Marcus returned. He looked far more happy now than when he left a few minutes earlier. "The marshals are coming back to the ranch with us. They will stay until this is all over. No matter how long it takes."

Emma didn't know whether to laugh or cry. The marshals might think they were doing the right thing, but they were no match for Tommy. The man is pure evil, and had gotten away with it for far too long. Shaking her head wasn't enough, but right now she had no words.

"Talk to me, Emma," Marcus said. She could hear the frustration in his voice. Marcus didn't know Tommy like she did. He would eliminate any obstacles in his way, which is likely what happened to the other witness.

"Tommy will kill you all. He won't care if some of the men are marshals. He'll eliminate anyone who gets in his way." Tears streamed down her face. "I couldn't bear to lose you, Marcus." Emma wasn't sure why she'd said those last words. Knowing a person for only a matter of days, didn't mean they had a connection. She had a glimmer of feelings toward the man who was now her husband, but there was no way she could be in love with him. Not after such a short time.

He was kind, gentle, and was looking out for her. That didn't mean much – he was kind to everyone. At least that's what she had seen. Which meant he didn't necessarily have feelings for her either.

Her mind was in a spin. She didn't know what to do. Going back to the ranch made sense, but then she took danger with her. Running also made sense, especially now her name was changed. Tommy could no longer locate her by the name on her stagecoach ticket. Using her real name had been stupid, but it was too late once it was done.

Of course she could go to another town by stagecoach, then change to a train. Where she would end up, Emma didn't know.

She shook her head again. None of it made sense right now. Emma knew she was panicking, and that wouldn't do. Never had she been able to think when in panic mode, and today was no different. "I…I can't think straight," she told Marcus, and he pulled her into his arms.

Emma felt safe being held by this man. She wished they could stay like this forever. Unfortunately, it simply wasn't possible.

Chapter Ten

Marcus tried to keep his concentration on the drive home, but his head was swirling with the current situation. Keeping Emma safe had to be his number one priority now. Having two marshals come to the ranch to help protect her took a lot of organizing, but it had to be done.

He requested reinforcements, and Marshal Holmes sent a telegraph requesting back-up, but whether they were sent remained to be seen.

Trying not to be noticed, Marcus glanced across at Emma. She was stoney-faced, and he was certain stress played a major role in that. Not that she'd been relaxed since arriving at the ranch, because she hadn't. Emma had been wound up from the moment he laid eyes on her. And honestly, who could blame her.

It was blatantly obvious the man chasing his wife, Tommy Yates, was a cold-blooded killer. "How are you doing?" he asked quietly. Not that he expected her to be joyful, but surely she was more relaxed now the marshals would be there to protect her?

"It's simply not safe," she said.

As Marcus glanced across at her, he couldn't help but notice her searching their surroundings. Did she think the disgraced sheriff would be hiding here in Mountain View? He supposed it was possible, but doubted the other man would have been able to locate her. Especially since she stowed away on his wagon.

"Are you alright?" Marcus asked quietly.

Despite looking as though she was about to burst into tears, Emma said she was. Marcus knew differently. "I have a gun on my hip, and a rifle under the seat," he said gently. "You are not in danger."

Her eyes opened wide. "I…I'm not scared," Emma said, her voice choked with emotion.

It was clear to Marcus she was more than scared, she was downright terrified. Instead of answering, he reached an arm around his new wife and pulled her close. His heart thudded. Already, he was breaking his own rule.

Marcus had no idea why he was so enamored by Emma, but he was. Never had he felt this way about a woman before. Neither of them were young – he was not that far from forty, and although he hadn't asked her age, Marcus guessed Emma to be only a few years younger than himself.

She'd never before married, he knew that much from the conversation they'd had with the preacher. If he'd been sneaky, he probably could have seen her age on the marriage register. Except that wasn't Marcus. If he wanted to know, he would ask.

Emma leaned her head on his shoulder, and it warmed his heart. Having her feel comfort from him was rewarding. Her hand came up and covered his hands as they held the reins. It sent a shiver down his spine, and warmth flooded his entire body. "It's alright to be scared," he whispered, and felt her nod against his shoulder. Another shiver went down his spine.

He had no right to react in this way. Marcus needed to keep his distance, otherwise he was certain to fall in love with the bride he didn't want. He shook his head, trying to clear the cobwebs Emma's nearness caused. It didn't work – not that he ever expected it would.

Now they were married, it seemed to change everything. Before they were two people thrown together by circumstances. Now they were legally joined by marriage.

Marcus knew the hardest thing would be resisting his new wife. Why he'd declared they would have a marriage of convenience, he had no idea. Whatever compelled him to say it, he didn't know. What

Marcus did know was he wanted to take the words back, but it was already too late.

Emma seemed happy enough with the arrangement, and if he was honest with himself, Marcus was not prepared for heartbreak when the danger was over. He was certain she would want to leave once that was the case.

He felt her shuffle closer to him, and it almost dissolved his resolve. Keeping his distance was the way to go. Without warning, they heard gunshots. The marshals were following behind them. Despite that, Marcus reached for his rifle. "Do you know how to use a gun?" he asked Emma.

"Not really," she said, panic clear in her voice.

He turned briefly to face her. His wife was ashen. Even worse than when she was back at the sheriff's office. That couldn't be good.

Without warning, the two marshals rode up beside them. "It wasn't Yates. Rather it was an outlaw, looking for easy prey."

"How can you be certain?" Emma demanded. She was shaking again, and Marcus held tight to the rifle, in case they were wrong.

"Mrs. Tyler," Marshal Holmes said. "We know it's a difficult time, but trust me, we saw this man up close. It wasn't Yates."

They had no choice but to believe the marshal. He had no reason to lie to them. Marcus didn't believe he would say it wasn't the murderous sheriff if it was. Once they arrived at the ranch, he would question them further. Away from Emma's hearing. She was worried enough as it was.

Emma stared into the trees. Did she think someone could be hiding there? She could be right, but with two lawman flanking their buggy, Marcus didn't think anyone would take the chance. Then again, didn't they moments ago have to defend themselves from attack?

Marcus was finally coming to the realization this situation may be far worse than he first believed. Still, he wouldn't change a thing. He would still have married Emma, and he most certainly would do everything in his power to protect her. Even if that meant losing his own life in the process.

~*~

It was pure relief on his part when Marcus pulled the buggy to a halt outside the ranch house. Gus appeared from the barn, and the two marshals alighted from their horses. He could see the curiosity on Gus's face, and needed to fill him in.

Before he could do that, he needed to help his new wife down from the buggy. He hurried around to her side, and went to help. The moment he did, Marcus paused. Would she slap his hands away?

Remembering her earlier annoyance had him unsure as to whether he should help.

Emma stood and tugged her skirts up. He knew this was to stop herself tripping as she alighted the buggy, but now her ankles were in clear view for all to see. Marcus didn't mind the view, but didn't want the other men seeing them as well. "Emma," he whispered loudly, then pointed at the hem of her skirts.

Her cheeks quickly turned pink, and she dropped her skirts. Now she would have to let him help her down. Marcus wondered if, unconsciously, that was his plan all along. He quickly dismissed the idea, and began to help his wife down the few steps.

She hurried up the steps of the ranch until he called to her. It was then she turned back, her cheeks still burning. Marcus followed her up, taking the steps two by two until he caught up with her. It was then he leaned down and swung her up into his arms. He opened the door, then carried her across the threshold. Something he thought he may never do.

As a confirmed bachelor, Marcus had not planned on marrying. Now that he was married, he needed to act appropriately, and that meant ensuring his new wife was happy.

Once inside, Marcus gently put Emma to the floor. His hands still around her waist, he studied her face. She truly was beautiful. He'd been a fool to demand a marriage of convenience. Would she allow him to change his mind?

Probably not, since she didn't really want to marry him to begin with. "Marcus," she said quietly. Then placed her hands over the top of his. The shiver that went down his spine brought Marcus back to reality. "I need you to let me go," she said, this time more firmly. "The fire needs stoking. I can't do it with you holding me here."

Emma took her hands away, and he truly wished she had left them there. "I'll do it," he told her. "Looks like I'd best bring in more wood as well." Without another word, Marcus strode over to the fireplace, and pushed the logs around. He threw a few pieces of kindling on the fire, to get it going again. When it took, he added some smaller logs, then stood again.

Heading outside for logs, he noticed Emma was still standing where he'd left her. The two marshals stood outside on the porch. Waiting to be invited inside?

It was then Marcus realized why Emma appeared surprised. Had she come to the same conclusion he had only moments ago? Emma's room would be needed for one of the marshals to sleep in. The only other empty bedroom would be required for the second marshal.

Emma would be relegated to the master bedroom. She seemed incredulous about the prospect.

Chapter Eleven

Emma's heart pounded at the realization she would be sleeping in not only the same room, but the very same bed as Marcus.

She had hoped for a real marriage with her new husband, but not under duress. Not when he was put in a position that forced them to sleep together. The mere fact this was happening told Emma the two marshals were unaware they had married that same morning. It also meant they were not told it was a marriage of convenience.

Not that she had insisted on that. Marcus had declared that it would be the case, and not given her a choice. Emma had dreamed of her fairytale wedding as a little girl. As she grew older, and had not found her Prince Charming, she had given up all hope of marrying. Now she was in her mid-thirties, Marcus was her last hope to have a real marriage and a family.

She had prayed for this day for as long as she could remember. His determination to keep his distance had taken all that away. Instead of brooding about it, Emma knew she needed to get on with things.

Marcus didn't want her as a real wife, and she had to accept it. Hurrying into what had been her room, Emma stripped the bed, and readied it for their guest. She checked the second bedroom. It was a little dusty, and the floor needed sweeping, but otherwise ready to accept it's guest.

She glanced out the window of the bedroom. Emma had to admit both rooms were perfect for the marshals. You could see almost the entire area in front of the ranch house. The barn was also in sight. That would surely mean no one could sneak into the house without being seen? It did reassure Emma of her safety with the two lawman staying there. Even if it put her in a difficult situation.

On hearing the front door slam, Emma hurried to the closet and extracted the broom. She quickly swept the floor of each room, to ensure they were ready for the men who would be her protectors until goodness knew when.

"If you're sure it's alright," Emma heard Marshal Holmes say.

The footsteps were getting closer. "Of course," Marcus replied, but he didn't sound certain. The trouble was, they had no choice. They couldn't relegate the marshals to the bunkhouse. What good would that do? They would take turns at protecting her, they'd said earlier. One would be there to protect her, and the other would sleep. There would be some crossover, and both would be around.

Emma knew exactly how dangerous Tommy Yates was, and hoped the lawmen understood that too.

She hurried out of the bedroom, past Marcus and the marshals. Heading for the pantry, Emma had to plan the evening's meal. Since it was so late in the day, it would have to be something that didn't require hours of cooking. In the meantime, she needed to prepare refreshments for her guests and the other men.

Thankfully she'd baked yesterday. She'd made a pound cake, as well as lemon muffins. They would suffice for today, but tomorrow Emma knew she would have to spend time baking again. Hard working men, like those on Marcus's ranch, required good food.

While the kettle heated up, she cut the pound cake, plating it and placed it in the center of the table. The muffins were also added to the table. All she needed to do now was take the mugs out of the cupboard and fill them with coffee.

Despite the stress of the day, glancing out the kitchen window helped to calm her. Emma loved it here on Marcus's ranch. It was peaceful, which helped to keep her calm. As much as she could be anyway. The wildflowers dancing in the breeze were so pretty, not to mention mesmerizing. Emma could stand there all day watching them.

Except she didn't have the time. The workers would be making their way back to the ranch by now. Marcus had told them this morning to come in for refreshments and an update. That meant she had seven hungry men to feed. Not only this afternoon, but also for however long it took for the marshals to capture Tommy Yates.

Looking back, the writing was on the wall. Tommy always enjoyed teasing and even harming the other boys. He didn't dare touch the girls – he knew the punishment for that. Emma always believed it was Tommy who had killed local kittens and other pets, but he never owned up when interviewed by his father, the sheriff at the time.

It was clear his father understood what Tommy was doing, but couldn't prove it. That was to the detriment of the entire town. Tommy had grown from a malicious child, into an evil adult. One who did not see life as sacred. Instead, he believed people were disposable, and snuffed out their lives at the slightest provocation. Or for no reason at all.

The thought made her shiver.

Two arms came up around her, and Emma screamed, her heart pounding in her head. Had Tommy found her already? "It's only me," Marcus whispered, and she relaxed against him. "I didn't mean to startle you." He turned her around in his arms and stared down into her face. "You were shaking," he said. "I decided you needed comforting."

Indeed she did, but the last thing Emma expected was for Marcus to pull her so close. Not that she didn't like it, because she did.

The sound of running reassured her the marshals were looking out for her. Even if she didn't need them in this instance.

"It's alright, gentlemen," Marcus told them. "I inadvertently startled my wife. Please accept my apologies," he said.

"Please, take a seat at the table," Emma told them. "Coffee will be ready shortly."

Both men muttered their thanks. Marcus stayed by Emma's side while she poured the coffee. They both added the mugs to the table, along with milk and sugar.

The other men would be here soon. She already felt protected. Having seven men looking out for her was beyond all expectations.

Now all Emma had to do was try to relax. Despite knowing her life was about to change forever.

~*~

Emma knew it wouldn't be easy. Going to bed when she knew Marcus would be there too. Sharing a bed with a man who was effectively a stranger, was not the way she envisaged her wedding night all those years ago.

Her plan was to find a man she liked. A man she would eventually love. They would marry, and *then* they would sleep together in the same bed. Everything was happening the wrong way around. After knowing Marcus for only a matter of days, she certainly liked him, but love wasn't even on her radar. She expected the same was true for him.

After supper, Emma, Marcus, and the marshals retreated to the sitting room. Marcus stoked the fire and made sure it had plenty of fuel to see out the night. It became quite chilly overnight at this time of year, according to her husband. Getting up to a cold house was not what any of them wanted.

Making sure their mugs were full of coffee, Emma sat down and enjoyed the heat from the fire. It was comforting, but also made her feel more tired than she already was. As she began to doze in her seat, the men, who kept their voices low, discussed her situation and what could be done to protect her.

It was upsetting to know somewhere out there, a man she knew well, wanted to kill her. Except Emma knew he wouldn't stop with her. Anyone in the vicinity would be a target. That meant, in one foul sweep, Tommy Yates would kill them all. Seven innocent lives lost. And all because she witnessed not one, but four brutal murders.

Chapter Twelve

Marcus didn't want to discuss strategies in front of his wife, but had no choice. They kept their voices low, hoping she wouldn't hear what they were discussing. When he glanced across, her eyes were closed, and Emma was sleeping.

He motioned for the others to wait, and the discussion stopped abruptly. "Emma," he said, trying not to startle her. That didn't work, so he gently shook her shoulder. Her eyes fluttered open, and stared up at him, despite her being in a sleep deprived stupor. Marcus wasn't certain she was really awake. "Why don't you go to bed?" he said firmly, and she nodded her head.

Helping his wife to her feet, Marcus walked her into the bedroom. The one he'd slept in alone for many years. He understood the position Emma had been forced into, and felt bad for her. It's not what either of them had signed up for. Still, the marshals needed to do their job, and needed to use the spare bedrooms.

Once in their room, he pulled the covers back. Emma was in no position to undress herself, but he had no intention of doing it either. Although technically, he was within his rights to do so. Instead he helped her onto the bed, and laid his wife down then removed her shoes. She was already sound asleep.

He carefully pulled the bedding up to cover her, then watched her sleep for several minutes. Never did he believe he'd be in this situation. Having a wife was not in his plans. Marcus finally slipped out of the room and closed the door without another sound.

"She's already asleep," he told the marshals, then resumed his seat.

Marshal Holmes spoke. "I'm not surprised," he said. "It's been a stressful day for her. You too, I'm sure."

Marcus didn't answer immediately, but took in the marshal's words instead. "Indeed, it has been," he finally said. He didn't anticipate the coming days to be any easier. "Emma is a strong woman, but this business has rattled her," he said. It had upset him too, but Marcus had no intention of admitting it. Besides, he was upset about his wife's situation, and nothing more.

"We need to discuss how this will work," Marshal Daniel Gregson said firmly.

Marcus nodded, then listened carefully, hugging his mug of coffee, and occasionally taking a mouthful of the now lukewarm beverage.

After outlining the plans, Marshal Peter Holmes added, "I'll take first shift," he said. "Daniel will take over in the morning after having a good night's sleep."

The three dispersed to go their separate ways. Peter stayed in the sitting room, gun on his hip. Daniel went to bed, and Marcus was conflicted. Should he stay out here with the marshal? Or join his new wife?

The thought of his warm and comfortable bed enticed him to go to his bed. Surely Emma would understand he had nowhere else to sleep? Except perhaps in one of the sitting room chairs, and they were far from comfortable for sleeping.

The bed it was. He crept into their bedroom, trying not to wake his wife in the process. He needn't have worried – she slept like the dead, not moving at all. Marcus undressed, and climbed into bed. He only hoped she didn't hold it against him come morning. Unfortunately, it was unavoidable.

As he lay his head on the pillow, Marcus glanced across at his wife. Warmth filled him, and Marcus knew things were not going the way he'd planned. Every time he was near her, or even when he so much as glanced in Emma's direction, he felt more enamored than the last time.

He'd got himself in a heap of trouble. And he wasn't talking about the Tommy Yates situation.

~*~

Marcus woke long before Emma did. He quickly dressed and left the room. "Morning, Marshal," he told Peter. "Anything to report?" He was concerned and sleep was fitful, even knowing there was a marshal keeping guard.

"Thankfully nothing," Peter Holmes told him. "Yates will likely drag this out, trying to catch us off-guard. I can assure you, it won't happen."

Marcus breathed a sigh of relief. They all needed to be on alert. Day and night. He acknowledged the marshal's words with a nod, then squatted down, stoked the sitting room fire and added logs to it, then stoked the cook-stove. Once that was going nicely, he filled the kettle with water.

He decided to let Emma sleep. She had been up before him from the first morning she was here. She'd made coffee, cooked a hearty breakfast, and cleaned up afterwards. Today it was his turn. The men would be disappointed, but there was nothing Marcus could do about it.

He went out to the hen house and gathered the eggs. If Emma could cook a decent breakfast, surely he could, too? Next he retrieved a piece of bacon, and began to slice it, ready for cooking. It was then he heard movement behind him and spun around.

Emma stood in the doorway, her hair still tussled from sleep, and her face soft with that just awake look. Marcus knew he would happily wake up to this each and every day. She stepped toward him, her determination now showing in her expression. "I can do that," she told him firmly. It made him smile.

He leaned in and whispered in her ear. "Perhaps you should clean up and get dressed first." The shocked look on her face told Marcus he'd startled her awake. Emma turned and ran out of the kitchen. He continued slicing the bacon. It wasn't like he'd not done this before, because he had. Many times since Cookie died.

He heard the bathroom door slam, then quiet. A few minutes later, his wife returned to the kitchen, her eyes wide open, her hair no longer disheveled. She wore one of her new gowns. "You look lovely," Marcus told her as Emma stepped over to the stove.

"I can take over now," she said, completely ignoring his comment. She reached into the cupboard for the large frying pan, and placed it on the stove to warm up. He should have done that when he first arrived in the kitchen. At least the kettle was boiling.

The front door opened, and the men began to take their places at the table. Emma served the coffee while Marcus finished slicing the bacon. The moment he did, Emma took over. "Sit down and enjoy your coffee," she said.

He knew he shouldn't, but Marcus wanted to wrap her in his arms in that moment. Instead he sat down and joined the banter at the table. Both marshals were there, having a low conversation between only them. Peter would be updating Daniel about the lack of activity last night, Marcus was certain.

The aroma of food cooking was something they hadn't had after the loss of Cookie, but Emma was certainly making up for that.

Marcus watched as Emma cooked. His offers of help refused, he had no choice but to sit at the table drinking coffee. His wife was organized, there was no doubt. It made him wonder if she'd worked in a restaurant or café at some point. Her cooking was far above anything he'd eaten before. Even Grace's food at the diner – and her cooking was excellent.

Emma had an elegance about her. Every movement seemed controlled, and every step she took, planned. It convinced him even more she had at some point, cooked professionally. Marcus shook himself mentally. Why he'd come to that conclusion, he didn't know.

Of course Emma was more graceful. Cookie was not Emma. He was a big man, and plodded his way through the job. He also wasn't a trained cook – he was self-taught, and did a far better job than the rest of them.

He studied her as Emma handed out the breakfasts. When it came to his turn, he stared up at his wife. "Thank you, Chef," he said. Where that had come from he didn't know, but the expression on her face was one of shock.

"How…" She shuddered. "How did you know?" she asked quietly.

Guilt filled him. He didn't even know why he'd said it. "It was a joke," he said. And it was. At least it was meant to be. "Does that mean you are a chef? You are so capable in the kitchen, it makes perfect sense." Marcus reached up and held her hand.

Emma nodded, then walked back to the stove to retrieve her own meal. When she took her place at the table, she didn't look at him. He'd done the wrong thing. He had called her out. If he'd done so with no one else there, it wouldn't have mattered. Did that mean he'd humiliated her? It wasn't his intent. Besides, she had nothing to be embarrassed about.

With breakfast over, Emma cleared the table and washed the dishes. Marcus checked the fire. Not only was the room warmed, his heart was filled with love and warmth. He hurried over to his wife. Now, more than ever, he wanted to spend as much time as possible with her. As she stood at the sink, he came up behind her and wrapped Emma in his arms. She leaned into him.

Marcus knew they shouldn't be doing this. Not if theirs was to be a loveless marriage. One of convenience.

Except he already knew in the short time they knew each other, it had grown into more than that. His heart fluttered at the thought of being with Emma for the rest of their lives. Loving Emma the way she deserved.

First though, they needed to eliminate the threat against her. Tommy Yates was out there somewhere. He was a deadly threat to Emma, and had to be stopped.

Chapter Thirteen

Emma could stand here in Marcus's arms all day if he'd let her. She felt safe when he was around. And loved.

He'd demanded a marriage of convenience, and by her silence, she'd agreed to those terms. When she woke up last night and came face to face with him, Emma knew a marriage of convenience would never work.

Not for either of them. His arm was wrapped around her waist, and he'd pulled her close. She made no attempt to pull away from Marcus, nor did she want to. He looked so peaceful in slumber, and it attracted her to him even more.

A lesser man would have handed her to the sheriff as soon as he'd found her in his barn. Not Marcus. He was compassionate and kind.

She could have ended up in a hostile environment. Emma now realized the stupidity of her actions. There was no way of knowing who owned that wagon, and she certainly wasn't in a position to find out. Getting away from Tommy Yates was her one and only goal. If he traced her to Mountain View, he would assume she'd continued on to the next town.

He always treated her like a fool. Emma was far from that.

As Marcus continued to hold her, Emma relaxed against him. She suddenly straightened. "I can't stand her like this all day," she said gruffly. "I have far too much to do." She shrugged out of his arms, and his warmth left her. Regret instantly filled her.

Marcus reached for her hands and held them tight. "You need to relax. Come and sit by the fire," he said as he stared into her eyes. He pulled her toward the sitting room. Thankfully, she had finished cleaning the kitchen, and ensured everything was where it should be.

After guiding her into a comfortable chair close to the warmth of the fire, Marcus sat in the chair closest to her. "I have to organize today's meals," she said. She heard the annoyance in her voice, and was certain Marcus would have too. "Don't you have work to do?" she asked quietly. This time ensuring her annoyance didn't show.

"I'm having time off to be with my bride," he said matter-of-factly. Then he smiled. A shiver went down her spine. It wasn't often he smiled, but when he did, it always affected her. Emma knew it shouldn't. She didn't want to get attached to a man who only married her to keep her safe. After Tommy was caught, what then? Would he ask for an annulment? Would he even give her a choice?

He stood then. "I'll be back in a minute. Wait here for me."

Marcus left the room, and true to his word, was back in no time. Suddenly the two marshals ran out the door. Marcus sat back down as though nothing was remiss.

"What's going on?" Emma asked, but was certain she already knew. "He's here, isn't he?" Her voice broke, and Emma was unable to hide the emotions that almost overwhelmed her.

"I'm not sure," Marcus told her. "I saw movement through the kitchen window. Better safe than sorry." He patted the gun on his hip, as though to reassure himself in case Tommy happened to get into the house.

Emma swallowed. She closed her eyes and took a deep breath, then let it out slowly. Not only was she at risk, now she'd put her husband at risk too. Not to mention the two marshals and four cowboys. Instead of killing only her, Tommy would kill six others in the process.

What's worse, he wouldn't flinch at the unnecessary deaths of seven people. It was something Emma couldn't fathom. Why did

Tommy kill at random? The only conclusion she could come to was the man was unhinged. Deranged.

From the day they'd met, Emma felt there was something wrong with Tommy. As time went on, she was convinced of it. Allowing him to become sheriff meant he'd turned a corner. His true level of wickedness finally appeared. She didn't have enough fingers to count the number of people he'd killed for no reason at all.

Emma's heart hammered. If he managed to get to the ranch house, it would be a massacre. Of that, she had no doubt.

~*~

As they waited for the two marshals to return, Emma's heart pounded. Tommy would not discriminate about who he eliminated to get to her. He would kill anyone who got in his way. Marcus tried to keep her calm – holding her hands helped a little, but her entire body was shaking. There was nothing he could do about that.

Suddenly the door flew open. Emma screamed, despite trying to keep her composure. "We couldn't find anyone or anything," Peter Holmes told them.

Daniel Gregson sat down next to Marcus. "We're putting it down to deer. We searched the area, but there was no one to be found. No human footprints in the snow either."

Marcus kept her hand in his. It was comforting, but Emma knew she couldn't expect him to always be by her side.

"I need to get some sleep," Peter said. "Daniel will wake me if necessary."

Once the marshal had left the room, Marcus turned to Daniel Gregson. "Are two marshals enough?" he asked, his hand never leaving Emma's.

"We've already requested additional marshals, but no idea when they'll arrive." Daniel sat down close to the fire. It was cold outside, and he was likely chilled to the bone.

Emma stood. "Coffee, anyone?" she asked, knowing full well both men would accept her offer. She was so confident, Emma made her way to the kitchen and pulled down the mugs before they had an opportunity to answer.

Despite her reservations, she glanced out the kitchen window. There was a smattering of snow everywhere. It wasn't heavy enough to build a snowman, but there was plenty of snow to make the area look magical.

If she wasn't being pursued by a killer, Emma knew she would enjoy the scenery. Instead her eyes scanned her surroundings, checking that Tommy wasn't anywhere close. She was about to turn away when she saw movement. She gasped, and put her hand to her chest. As she watched, her heart beat faster than before. Emma froze.

Chapter Fourteen

Marcus heard Emma gasp and ran to her side. Daniel was on his heels.

The two men followed her gaze. Both marshals had checked the area only minutes ago. There couldn't be anything there now, surely? Except Marcus suspected Tommy Yates was an expert at hiding his whereabouts. Especially as he'd been a sheriff for many years.

How the authorities had not done something about the malicious sheriff, he had no idea. Finally they had proof and could lock him away. That was, provided they could find and catch him. Marcus didn't like the fact his wife was being used as bait to catch Yates.

Not that the marshals would admit such a dastardly thing, but Marcus was certain that was their plan. Putting her under their protection would make far more sense, but it likely wouldn't catch the killer.

Particularly since Peter Holmes confided his suspicion the man was deranged. It made perfect sense. Why else would a sheriff kill random people?

According to Emma, it had been going on for years. Which again begged the question, *why was he not stopped?*

"I promise you," Daniel said, "we will protect you with our lives. Ah, see?" he added. "It's a buck."

Marcus was relieved and knew Emma would be too, except the danger was still there. "We don't often get deer out this way," he told the marshal. "But I'm certainly glad we have solved the mystery."

Emma poured the coffee and placed their mugs on the table. She endeavored to pull down a tin from a high cupboard, and Marcus noticed her struggling. Standing behind her, he reached it easily and handed it to Emma. That freed his hands to wrap them around her. She didn't push him away.

He watched as she attempted to cut the pound cake. Her hands trembled. Emma was more shaken than she let on. "Let me," he said gently. She nodded, and moved out of his embrace.

Once the cake was sliced and on the table, he turned to face his wife. She stood at the window staring out. He couldn't begin to imagine what she was facing, nor how she was feeling. Despite that, she seemed to function well under the pressure. Most of the time.

Emma had buttered her bread, the others followed suit. They might be rough and ready cowboys, but they had manners.

Marcus decided happy Emma was the only side of his wife he wanted to see. He hated seeing her unhappy and frightened. It wasn't right she should be in this position because of a man who killed whomever got in his way.

"The food is delicious, as always," Marcus said. He'd almost said *sweetheart*, but stopped himself in time. Every day they were together became more difficult for Marcus to keep his distance. He had to admit it was already too late. He was at his happiest around Emma, and she seemed to feel the same way.

When everyone finished their food, Emma stood. "Anyone for seconds?" she asked, and headed toward the stove and the large pot of soup without waiting for an answer. She was now used to these men and their needs. Emma made certain they ate well, with fresh food created daily. There were rarely any leftovers. When there were, the chickens made short work of them.

"What's for supper?" Cody, one of the cowboys, asked.

Marcus glared at him. They hadn't finished lunch yet, and he was already worried about supper? Emma's hand went to his shoulder. "Roast chicken with roasted vegetables," she told him. "I'm not sure about dessert yet."

Marcus knew otherwise. Emma had her meals planned for at least a day ahead. She'd told him it's what she did in the café. It was probably far more important here at the ranch, since she didn't have a mercantile nearby to get supplies at short notice. He reached under the table and squeezed her hand.

Turning to face him, Emma threw him the biggest smile. His heart fluttered, and warmth flooded him. "However," she said, turning to Cody again. "I do have apple pie for lunch."

The table erupted – whoops, laughter and words of thanks. Emma knew exactly how to win the hearts of his men. Too bad for them she was already taken.

Chapter Fifteen

The moment she finished cleaning the kitchen from lunch, Emma was ready for a bit of relaxation. The kettle had boiled, and she was in the midst of making hot beverages for Marcus, Daniel, and herself.

"We have company," Emma said, her eyes never leaving the two men on horseback.

Daniel was by her side in moments, along with Marcus. His hand on his gun, Daniel studied the strangers, then let out a long breath. "They're marshals," he said, his relief evident. "I'll go and meet them outside."

Emma was far more relieved than she thought she would be. Having two marshals nearby meant she felt more protected. Four marshals would surely make her feel even better. It should also take a lot of pressure off Peter and Daniel.

Marcus put an arm around her, and kissed Emma's forehead. "It will be alright," he said gently. "I cannot see Yates even attempting to come here. He must know you are being protected."

Emma shook her head. Did he not understand? Tommy Yates was afraid of no one. If there were a dozen marshals here, Tommy would still try and penetrate their protective circle. "I'm certain he does," she whispered. "He's out there somewhere." Emma lifted a hand and pointed to the open space in front of them. She shuddered, and Marcus pulled her tighter toward him. "I can feel his presence."

Marcus stared down into her face. He lifted his hand and caressed her cheek. "If he was there, the marshals would know."

As determined as Marcus was, Emma knew better. There were plenty of places for Tommy to hide. He was a master at hiding from view. It was one of the ways he was able to kill his prey. Emma shivered again. The realization that *she* was his prey this time, suddenly hit her.

The front door opening startled her, and Emma jumped. This time Marcus wrapped her in his arms. It must pain him to be comforting her this way, when he'd declared their marriage to be fake. How she allowed herself to marry a man who wasn't interested in her, Emma didn't know.

Except she did know. She was so desperate to get away from Tommy Yates, she'd seized on the first opportunity to come along. As she allowed herself to sink into her husband's chest, Emma finally understood how very lucky she was.

"Marcus, Emma," Daniel said, ushering the two newcomers into the kitchen. "This is Virgil and Ernie. The two marshals we've been expecting."

Marcus shook hands with both men, while Emma acknowledged them both. "I was about to make coffee when you arrived," she said. "Would you like some?"

"We would surely appreciate it," Virgil said. "It's been a long day, Ma'am." He removed his hat and coat, and Emma indicated for both men to take a seat at the table.

Reaching for two more mugs, Emma felt far more protected now. With four marshals here, there would be two for each watch. It was as though her worries were gone, knowing Tommy would not get away with his murderous sprees.

Emma reached for the tray of muffins she'd made earlier and plated them up. The wild blueberries that grew at the end of the porch meant she could add them to muffins, to cakes, and even make jelly with them. Marcus told her there was an abundance of blackberries too, but they didn't have her quite so excited.

Adding the muffins to a large plate, she placed them in the middle of the table. "They are still warm," she told the newcomers. "You arrived at the right time." She smiled then, and Marcus reached for her.

"Didn't I tell you?" he whispered, "It will all turn out fine." Emma stared up into his face. He appeared more relaxed than earlier. It seemed the two additional marshals made them both feel more secure.

~*~

"I hope we're not an added burden, Ma'am," Virgil told Emma as she checked the roasting chickens.

"Not at all. There is more than enough for everyone. And please, call me Emma." After basting the chickens and returning them to the oven, Emma headed to the root cellar.

"Ma'am, Emma," Virgil called. "I will accompany you."

Glancing at Marcus, Emma knew he wasn't happy. After all, neither of them knew this man. He might be a marshal, but was he safe to be alone with? "I'm coming too," Marcus said. "I…I need to check the supplies."

Breathing a sigh of relief, Emma showed Virgil where the root cellar was located. The marshal went in first, then Emma, and lastly Marcus.

"I needed to ensure there was no other entry into the root cellar," Virgil said. He turned to Emma. "Thankfully, there isn't. Unless it's hidden?"

"Not hidden. There is only one way in," Marcus told him.

"If Yates breaches the property, both of you head straight down here. I don't want either of you to be a target."

The tone of his voice told Emma the marshal would not allow defiance of his orders. He certainly seemed to know what he was doing, and seemed to be in charge of the four marshals there.

Emma picked the vegetables she needed and added them to the basket she'd taken to the root cellar. The three headed back upstairs, Marcus held her back momentarily while Virgil went first. He sent Emma next, but when she looked back, noticed he'd turned his head away. Always the gentleman, Marcus had ensured neither himself nor Virgil had the opportunity to see up her dress. The thought had her heart fluttering.

The moment she was back in the kitchen, Emma peeled and cut the vegetables to be roasted. Thankfully, the root cellar held more than enough for tonight's supper. She estimated there would be enough for several days. Maybe longer, depending on what meals she decided on for the next few days.

Right now though, she merely wanted to get through today. She would worry about tomorrow in the morning. That was, if she was still alive to make decisions.

Chapter Sixteen

The days felt to be drawn out. Normally Marcus would be out with his men working. It didn't seem right to leave Emma alone with four men, none of whom they knew. Not really.

Besides, there was no way he would go while she was in danger. Emma was far more important to him than the ranch. As much as Tommy Yates was the enemy, boredom was also against him. The only thing that kept Marcus sane, was spending time with Emma.

She sat at the table sipping tea, and working out menus. She appeared happy enough doing so, and he guessed it brought some form of normality to her days. Every now and then, Emma would jump up and hurry into the pantry. It had taken a while, but he finally realized she was checking supplies.

As she returned once more to her list, Emma announced nonchalantly, *he's here*, then went back to her menus.

Marshals Ernie and Virgil ran to her side. "What do you mean, he's here?" Virgil demanded.

"I can feel his presence," Emma told him. "A quick check out the kitchen window should confirm what I said. Tommy is not one to hide unnecessarily."

Both Marshals ran to the kitchen window. "Well, I'll be…" Virgil muttered under his breath. "Get Daniel and Peter. The fool has finally shown himself."

Marcus wandered over to their sides. "Why would he stand there in broad daylight?" he asked, completely confused. "Apart from the fact the man is deranged," he added.

Emma joined the others and stared at the killer who stood in the middle of the field, staring back at them. "He believes himself to be invincible. He has killed so many people without repercussions," she said. "Why would he not believe it?" She turned to go back to her menus, but changed her mind. "I wouldn't stand there too long. He's just as likely to open fire." Finally she went back to the table.

His wife's words shook Marcus to the core. It appeared none of them realized who they were dealing with. Emma knew him well, so it was imperative they heeded her words.

No longer the frightened woman who had hidden in the back of his wagon, then slept in his loft, her demeanor was one of complete and utter calm. Marcus wasn't certain what worried him more – her apparent indifferent attitude of possible death, or the fact Tommy Yates had now shown himself.

"You two, into the root cellar," Virgil demanded.

Emma studied the marshal. "I'm not going anywhere. Tommy isn't stupid – he won't get close enough for you to either kill or arrest him. It's me he wants. Let me coax him out."

Marcus's heart hammered. He was rendered speechless. How could Emma even think that way? It was bad enough when he thought the marshals were using her as bait. But offering herself up to entice Yates out? "No," he said firmly, then reached for her hand. Emma pulled it away.

"We need this to be over," she told him gently. "Neither of us can continue to live like this. I don't know about you, but I've barely slept since arriving here."

Emma was right, of course she was. Marcus tossed and turned most nights. Waiting for Yates to breach the house and kill them all was always on the cards. When you have a cold-blooded killer as he was, combined with the man being deranged, anything could happen.

Without another word, Emma stood. After pouring a fresh cup of tea, she headed to the front door. Marcus followed her. "Emma, wait!" he demanded, but she ignored his plea. Hand on the door handle, she paused momentarily. Was she having second thoughts? He certainly hoped so.

A firm hand to his shoulder alerted Marcus the marshals understood. "Let her go," Virgil said. "She will draw him out. I promise you, no harm will come to your wife."

A promise was a promise, but in this case, Marcus wasn't convinced Virgil could make such a statement.

"Yates is moving. He's heading toward the porch," Ernie called.

Marcus couldn't believe what was happening. "Please don't do this," He begged Virgil. "I love my wife. I can't live without her." His words shocked Marcus. He already knew he had feelings for Emma, but over time she'd become far more than he'd even believed possible. More important than anything or anyone else. His eyes filled with tears. It had been a long time since he'd cried over anyone. The last time was when he lost his parents all those years ago.

"We have her covered. Now let us do our job." Virgil indicated for Marcus to go sit down in the sitting room, but he was having none of that.

Without another word, Marcus ran for the door, and joined his wife on the porch. He sat down beside her as though nothing was amiss. Emma glanced up at him, a scowl on her face. "What are you doing out here?" she whispered. Instead of answering, he reached for her hand. "Well?" she demanded. "Go back inside."

Marcus took a long fortifying breath then let it out slowly. He squeezed Emma's hand, and said the words he should have said long ago. "Emma Tyler, I love you," he said. "I can't imagine my life without you. If Yates kills you, he has to kill me too." A tear slid down his face at the thought of not having Emma by his side for the rest of their lives. This time he didn't try to hide his emotions.

Emma leaned over and kissed him. Marcus's heart fluttered, then he kissed her back. Not a peck on the cheek, or the forehead as he'd done in the past, but on her lips. The lips he'd longed to kiss for far too long. "I love you, too," she whispered.

"That's wonderful." The voice reeked of sarcasm.

Marcus's head shot up. His heart hammered, and he held Emma's hand. This was it. Tommy Yates had finally shown himself.

"Tommy. How are you?" Emma said as though she was greeting a long lost friend.

Yates lifted his gun. First he aimed it at Marcus, then at Emma. "Better than you," Yates said sarcastically.

The sound of gunshots echoed in Marcus's ears.

Chapter Seventeen

Emma's heart pounded as Tommy lifted the gun and aimed it toward Marcus. She couldn't bear if he killed Marcus just to spite her. Tommy was like that, always had been.

The ringing in her ears was palpable, and tears filled her eyes. *She* was meant to be the bait, not Marcus. Not the man who hid her all this time. They might not have been together very long, but she loved him dearly. Emma didn't want to see Marcus – she preferred to remember him as a live, wonderful human. The man she married, and now loved with all her heart.

As her ears continued to ring, Emma closed her eyes. Tommy would kill her too, and it would be a blessed relief. She couldn't live with the knowledge she had brought danger to the Mountain View Ranch.

She knew it was a risk coming out here to the porch, but it had to be done. Tommy needed to be stopped, otherwise he would keep on killing. If that meant she lost her life in the process, so be it.

Everything seemed to move in slow motion. Was that how things seemed when you'd been shot? The strange thing was she didn't feel the bullet hit. Emma knew she'd been shot because of the moisture. Her chest was covered in blood. It's warmth somehow comforting.

She heard the door slam shut behind her. Muffled voices followed. Intense ringing in her ears meant she had no idea what was going on around her. The next thing Emma knew, she was being lifted. The hands were gentle, yet strong. A tender kiss to her cheek had her feeling grateful. Moments later, it felt as though she was floating on a cloud of feathers.

"Emma," a muffled voice said. "Open your eyes." Was she in heaven? There was no doubt she was dead – Tommy never missed his target. Not ever. "It's over. Tommy Yates is dead," Marcus said, then kissed her cheek again.

Glancing up, Emma saw Marcus. They were together again. That made her happy. "I'm sorry," she whispered, then closed her eyes again.

"Emma, you're alive. I'm alive. Tommy Yates is dead."

The ringing in her ears began to clear. "Tommy is dead? And we're alive? But…what is all this blood?" she asked, feeling more than a little confused.

"Not blood, Ma'am," Virgil told her. "It's tea."

Emma felt like laughing. She spilled her tea? A man was dead, but she wanted to celebrate. Her mind was in confusion. First though, she needed to know. "Was anyone else….hurt?" She swallowed down the emotions that had surfaced at the news her pursuer could no longer make her life hell.

"Not a soul, Ma'am," Virgil said, then left the room.

It had been an eventful day, and Emma wanted nothing more than to put it behind her. Life had to go on, but it left a sour taste in her mouth. She already had a stew on the stove when Tommy had turned up, and now she was dishing it up to the hungry men sitting around the table.

Once everyone was served, Emma sat next to her husband. "Before we begin eating, I want to thank you. Each and every one of you has made my life better." Her gaze went from one to the other. Emma wanted each man to know how much she appreciated them. Virgil and Ernie had already left, taking Tommy's body with them. Daniel and Peter would leave in the morning.

"No thanks needed, Emma," Daniel said firmly. "We did what had to be done."

She studied him, then licked her lips. There was still a question she needed answered. "Who…" Emma closed her eyes momentarily. "Who killed him? Am I allowed to know?" Marcus squeezed her hand, and Emma felt the hollowness in her chest begin to fill.

"He had four bullets to the chest. Each of the marshals shot him simultaneously." Peter studied her, then spoke again. "It was nothing less than he deserved."

Emma was grateful she didn't have to see his dead body, although it may have given her some closure. She had to believe what she was told, that Tommy Yates was no longer a threat to her or to anyone else.

"Thank you," she whispered, then picked up her fork. For the first time in weeks, she was genuinely hungry.

Epilogue

Three years later...

Marcus strode into the house, removing his hat as he entered. Emma was in the sitting room, feeding five month old baby Louisa.

Little Jake, who was now two, sat quietly playing with his toys. His son took after his mother. He was quiet and reserved, but only for now. Once Jake was old enough, he already had plans to buy the boy a pony. One day this ranch would be handed down to him. It was up to Marcus to ensure the boy was ready when he came of age. He would take Jake under his wing and teach him all there was to know.

The aroma permeating the room warmed Marcus. Emma was the best cook he'd ever come across. Even while she was pregnant with both their children, she cooked up a storm. He glanced across to the kitchen counter. Already Emma had begun to prepare for Christmas.

Marcus knew he was spoiled, and so were the cowboys. He couldn't think of a single ranch where they had chef cooked meals. Except the Mountain View Ranch, of course.

One thing he did know, and Marcus was truly grateful for it. The day Emma stumbled into his wagon, of all the wagons she could have chosen, was the best day of his life. Until then, he was going through the motions. He came alive almost the moment he found Emma in the loft, asleep in the hay.

He leaned down and kissed Louisa's forehead, then kissed Emma's lips. Although the kiss was brief, it sent a thrill down his spine. "How did I get so lucky?" he whispered, trying not to disturb the feeding baby.

Emma glanced up at him and smiled. "How did *I* get so lucky? Is that what you mean?" She lightly chuckled, and caressed the baby's cheek.

"Me too, Papa," Jake said, his arms outstretched toward his father. Marcus picked the boy up and held him tight.

His heart fluttered. A little over three years ago, he would never have believed he would have a family now. If anyone had said he would be happily married, Marcus would have laughed in their face.

Except that's exactly what his life was now. He glanced across at Emma, who now had the baby on her shoulder. "Marcus," she whispered. "Come here."

Taking his son with him, Marcus went to sit beside Emma. She smiled at him, her eyes sparkling, then reached for his hand. The moment she put it on her tummy, Marcus knew their little family was expanding again.

~*~

Christmas day was magical.

It was the first Christmas Jake was old enough to understand it was special, and not like every other day.

Emma had risen early to prepare the turkey and place it in the oven. Later, she would boil the plum pudding to heat it up ready for dessert.

Marcus turned at the knock on the front door. "Come in," he called. He couldn't control his excitement at seeing their four marshal friends again. After what they'd all endured at the hands of Tommy Yates, the marshals, Emma and Marcus had become friends. They were on a perpetual invitation to visit anytime, and Emma insisted they spend Christmas at the ranch. They were the closest to family for the marshals, as they had no family of their own.

"This can't be little Jake," Virgil said, his astonishment clear. "The boy has grown since we saw him last."

Marcus chuckled. "He definitely has. You haven't met our daughter, Louisa, yet." Right on cue, the baby woke from her nap and let out an almighty cry.

Emma left the room and returned with Louisa a few minutes later. "It is so good to see you all," she said, hugging each man, before turning to Marcus. "Can you take her while I check the turkey?" she asked, not waiting for an answer.

"The food smells amazing," Daniel said. "I knew there was a reason we keep coming back." He laughed, along with the other marshals.

Marcus herded them into the sitting room. "We best get out of Emma's way," he said, then lowered his voice. "She can be a bit grumpy when she's pregnant."

Virgil was the first to react. "You have another baby on the way? Congratulations to you both." He grinned, and Marcus knew his friend was pleased for them both. "Oh, before I forget, we have a gift for young Jake. It's outside."

"You shouldn't have," Marcus said and genuinely meant it. He'd told them the same thing last Christmas too, but they were determined to spoil the child.

"It's on the porch. Getting it here was tricky." Virgil said.

Marcus was curious to see what it was.

"Master Jake," Virgil called, and the boy ran to him. "Wait here with your Papa. We have a surprise for you." The marshals all filed outside. It wasn't long before they returned, all helping to carry the gift.

"It's a horsie," Jake exclaimed on seeing the wooden rocking horse.

"How…how did you get that here?" Marcus wanted to know. There was no way they could carry it on horseback.

"We had it shipped by train, then hired a wagon to get it out here," Ernie told him. "Where there's a will,"

"There's a way," Peter finished.

Jake ran to the rocking horse but needed help to climb up. "It won't be long and he'll be big enough to get up by himself," Virgil said.

The door opened and the four cowboys strolled in. "Just in time," Emma told them. "Everyone take a seat at the table."

With Jake balanced on his knee, Virgil sat proudly. Louisa seemed content in Marcus's arms for the moment. And everyone Marcus loved and respected was here in their home, sharing the most important day of the year.

From the Author

Thank you so much for reading my book – I hope you enjoyed it.

I would greatly appreciate you leaving a review where you purchased, even if it is only a one-liner. It helps to have my books more visible!

About the Author

Multi-published, award-winning and bestselling author Cheryl Wright, former secretary, debt collector, account manager, writing coach, and shopping tour hostess, loves reading.

She writes historical romantic suspense and historical western romance.

She lives in Melbourne, Australia, and is married with two adult children and has six grandchildren, and twin great-grandchildren.

When she's not writing, she can be found in her craft room making greeting cards.

Links

Website: *http://www.cheryl-wright.com/*

Facebook Reader Group:
https://www.facebook.com/groups/cherylwrightaut hor/

Join My Newsletter:

https://cheryl-wright.com/newsletter/
(and receive a free book)